STRANGE LITTLE GIRL

A DCI John Blizzard murder mystery

JOHN DEAN

THE
BOOK
FOLKS

Paperback published by The Book Folks

London, 2017

© John Dean

ISBN 978-1-9734-6213-2

www.thebookfolks.com

Strange Little Girl is the second book in a series of British murder mysteries featuring Detective Chief Inspector John Blizzard. Head to the back of this book for details of the author's other titles.

Chapter one

John Blizzard stared bleakly at the red paint that had been thrown over the gravestone. Kids, he thought. Whatever happened to respect for the dead? The question was quickly replaced by a more sinister one. The attacker could have used any coloured paint, so why choose red? To resemble blood, he decided. And why this gravestone of all the hundreds in Hafton Cemetery? And why this day of all days? Just a coincidence? No, concluded the detective chief inspector with a shake of the head, this was more than kids mucking about, this was someone with a message for the world. Or perhaps just for the police. For Blizzard. Or perhaps, he thought, someone with a message for Danny Galston, a reminder that his act had not been forgotten. For some in the city the emotions were as raw now as they were the day the murders were committed. Old memories die hard and Blizzard knew from personal experience that these died harder than most.

He reached out a hand and, on discovering that the paint was still wet, turned sharply to peer across the cemetery, seeking movement among the drooping trees. A flash of blue caught his attention at the far end of one of the paths, over by the crematorium. It revealed itself as an elderly woman shuffling along the long line of flowers laid out on the pavement after that day's funerals, the sharp late afternoon sunlight catching her coat. Occasionally, she crouched to read the dedication cards, reaching out to run a finger slowly over the words as if spelling them out. As the chief inspector watched, the pensioner looked round furtively then, with a surprisingly rapid movement for one of such advanced years, shot out a hand and snatched a small bunch of roses. Glancing round again, she straightened up and walked briskly in the direction of the cemetery gates, clutching her prize. Blizzard could not help chuckling; better the flowers brighten up her living room than wither away outside the crematorium. Looking across the cemetery, he noticed a woman in a headscarf. She was too far away for him to be sure but Blizzard sensed that she, too, had seen the incident and was smiling as well. She looked in his direction, and for a split second it seemed that they connected. Then she turned and was gone.

Blizzard turned back to the vandalised grave, which lay in an overgrown corner of the cemetery, beneath a large oak tree. He glanced at the neighbouring graves stretched along the nearby red-brick perimeter wall, half-concealed in shadows cast by the late afternoon sunlight. Most dated from the late 1800s, stained green with creeping lichens, their inscriptions all but obliterated by the scouring action of more than a hundred years of driving northern rains. Satisfying himself that none of them had been violated, Blizzard turned back to the only one that had. Violated was the word, he thought, as he surveyed the spattered paint. This was a calculated attempt to desecrate. But desecrate what? Desecrate whom? Desecrate Jenny Galston, who fought so hard to protect her children? Desecrate the memory of poor little Chloe? Dear God, surely not, he thought.

Blizzard looked pensively at the white lettering on the stone, the words bright and sharp against the shiny black marble. Not that the chief inspector needed to read the inscription, he knew well enough what it said:

Jenny Galston
Born July 9, 1973
Died November 13, 2002
Aged 29

And written beneath, next to a small picture of a cherubic little child, all brown curly locks and beaming smile:

Chloe Galston
Born April 4, 1995
Died November 13, 2002
Aged 7

Together for eternity. Rest in peace in the arms of the Lord.

Peace, thought Blizzard bitterly, there had been precious little of that in the last moments for mother and daughter. As always when he looked at the stone – and he never missed an anniversary of the deaths – the chief inspector was struck by the fact there was no mention of Pauline Galston. But then how could there be? Chloe's ten-year-old sister had somehow escaped the butchery of that night. Or at least, her body had never been found. She was still out there somewhere, either mouldering in the damp ground or walking around laden down with her memories. Or with no memories at all, perhaps? Blizzard did not know the answer and the thought disturbed him. It had always disturbed him. A veteran of many a murder case, this was one of the few that had found a way through his defences and there were still too many unanswered questions even fifteen years later. The Americans called it closure, John Blizzard preferred to call it unfinished business.

Standing in the peace of the cemetery, the light starting to fade as dusk approached, his mind went back to the events of that wicked night in Kensington Terrace, a

Victorian street not far from the city centre and on the very edge of Western CID's patch. Sometimes – many times – he wished he could not remember the events but he knew the images would never go away. Sometimes they shook him roughly from sleep and he would wake, sweating profusely, his heart thumping. A detective sergeant at the time, Blizzard had been the first CID officer to arrive at the house, police having been called shortly after 7.15pm following a frantic 999 call from a neighbour. He recalled once again his growing sense of horror as he entered the dimly-lit hallway to see the blood smeared along the linoleum floor. He recalled the young uniform constable sitting at the bottom of the stairs, her face ashen and hands gripping the banister for support, and he recalled the sound of an unseen male colleague throwing up in the downstairs bathroom at the back of the house.

The chief inspector tasted once more his own fear, sharp at the back of his throat. He remembered again how, hardly daring to breathe, he walked into the living room to find Jenny Galston, soaked in blood, dead from numerous knife slashes, hands thrown up to protect herself from her assailant, a mother fighting desperately to the last to protect her children. Chloe was upstairs, lying on her bloodstained bed, her curls smeared with blood; her clear blue eyes lifeless, and her bright green dress stained maroon. Blizzard had always remembered the motif on the front of the dress: a bright yellow elephant with sparkling eyes and a sparkly green hat, the animal still waving cheerily amid the carnage. Blizzard had stood in the bedroom and sobbed like he had never sobbed before, closing the door lest anyone see his tears. Not that they would have begrudged him his emotions – many were crying already, many more would cry time and time again for little Chloe in the years that would follow. Blizzard was one of them and he felt the tears start in his eyes again now.

'Damn,' he murmured, reaching into the trouser pocket of his suit and fishing out a white handkerchief. 'Damn, damn, damn.'

It never leaves you, he thought as he dabbed his eyes. That's what Harry Roberts used to say. Blizzard recalled his old friend and mentor, the detective chief inspector in charge of the initial investigation, standing in Chloe's bedroom, shaking his head in disbelief as he murmured over and over again, 'such savagery, such savagery.' Despite his determination to catch the killer, Harry Roberts was destined never to arrest him, taking his sense of guilt and failure to his own grave five years later, just three months before he was due to retire. Blizzard recalled that final evening in the darkened room of the hospice, as his friend lay dying of cancer, the Galston case the only unsolved murder in an outstanding career.

'John,' Blizzard recalled Harry saying, reaching out a frail hand from his bed, each painful word sending spasms through his withered body, 'get him for me.' Blizzard had nodded and, fighting back the tears, said hoarsely, 'I will, Harry, I will.' Harry had fallen silent after that and Blizzard had sat for an hour, holding his hand and crying silently in the darkness. Just before he left, assuming his friend to be asleep, Harry had squeezed his hand, whispering so quietly as to be almost inaudible, the words, 'I pray they can forgive me.' 'For what?' Blizzard had asked but there were no more words after that and he knew it was goodbye. By the time the night was over, Harry Roberts had found the peace that had eluded his final days.

Blizzard had not found that peace yet and the passing years had made his pledge to Harry seem a hollow one, that last cryptic comment as impossible to fathom now as it was at the time. Even now, having become the DCI in charge of the case four years previously, an arrest remained frustratingly distant for Blizzard, also the only unsolved murder case on the chief inspector's books. Well, Blizzard thought with an involuntarily shake of the head as he looked again at the gravestone, the official records might list the case as unsolved but he knew who had done it; everyone knew, even Harry had known. Always look close to home, Harry constantly told his officers, and close to home meant the children's father Danny Galston. Harry had never wavered from his belief about Galston's guilt and neither had John Blizzard. Sometimes the chief inspector would glance up to the heavens and wonder if Harry were watching him, urging him to make the breakthrough, force Danny Galston into that final mistake. The chief inspector did it now, staring up at the clouds that were starting to gather as the afternoon came to an end.

'Sorry, old son,' he murmured.

He hoped Harry heard. Somehow, he felt he had. Reaching down to place his flowers, Blizzard's thoughts turned back to Pauline Galston. He remembered, with a stab of guilt, that he had not cried for her. Neither had others on the inquiry, as far as he was aware. He knew why. Photographs showed a sallow child with long, lank black hair and staring, lifeless, eyes. She was, neighbours had said, a strange little girl. Solitary. Uncommunicative. Difficult to know. When they were talking to her, those eyes would shift away from their gaze and she would stare at the ground, apparently not hearing their words. By the time she reached her ninth birthday, Pauline hardly spoke to anyone and her teachers were expressing growing concern about her performance at school. Because she was different, the other children bullied and insulted her and, finally, having elicited no response and seeking more responsive targets, carried out their final indignity and left her to live in a world apart. Then on the night of November 13, 2002, Pauline Galston lived no more; even though her remains had never been found, Blizzard had always known instinctively she was dead. He had always felt the gravestone should have her name on it as well.

Glancing round at the sound of a cracking twig, he was not surprised to see a tall figure in a black windcheater picking his way across the damp grass, occasionally reaching out an arm to push through the bushes which had all but obscured some of the older graves. David Colley never missed an anniversary either, the detective sergeant drawn back by memories of those terrible events in his early days as a DC. The friends never made a formal arrangement to meet at the cemetery but both knew the other would be there at some time during the day.

'What happened?' asked Colley. He gestured at the paint. 'Kids?'

'Maybe.'

'You thinking something else?'

Blizzard shrugged. Colley placed his flowers alongside those of the chief inspector. Neither man said anything as they looked at the headstone in solemn silence. For Colley, the moment had additional poignancy because his girlfriend, Jay, was in the early weeks of pregnancy although the couple had not yet announced the news. Even though he and Blizzard had known each other for years, the sergeant dreaded telling him because he was not sure how he would react. Divorced from a childless marriage more than a decade ago, the chief inspector had never shown much empathy for children. Although Blizzard always tried to accommodate the demands that children placed on his officers, Colley sensed he did not really understand them. Indeed, it was only now that the sergeant was starting to appreciate the responsibilities that came with fatherhood. He realised it had been a hidden world, and as more of it was revealed to him, it grew ever more intimidating. The thought of little Chloe lying cold in the ground made it even more so for the sergeant. Never a particularly emotional man, he was surprised to feel the sting of tears and turned away so Blizzard could not see.

'You OK?' asked the chief inspector.

'Yeah, something in my eye.'

'Right.'

The men stood in silence for a few moments more, then Colley turned to his colleague.

'I'm beginning to suspect we'll never get him, guv.'

'We have to, otherwise I'll have to keep out of Harry's way when I get to heaven.'

'Who said you were going to heaven?'

Blizzard chuckled. A sudden breeze sprung up as the fading sun was blotted out by a cloud and a chill darkness descended on the cemetery. Startled, the chief inspector shivered and turned sharply, sensing someone behind him. Standing twenty metres away, between two weathered gravestones, was a young girl with long black hair. Wearing a white dress and probably no more than ten-years-old, she stared silently at the chief inspector with lifeless eyes.

'Jesus,' gasped Blizzard, the colour draining from his cheeks.

'What?' asked the sergeant, turning quickly.

'Don't you see her?'

Colley looked across the deserted cemetery to where his colleague was pointing.

'See who, guv?'

But she was gone.

Chapter two

The next morning found John Blizzard sitting in his office, deep in thought as he sipped his tea. It was seven o'clock and he had come into work early after a disturbed night in which the image of the strange little girl kept invading his dreams. Weary of his constant tossing and turning, his girlfriend Fee had kicked him out of bed shortly before five with orders to sleep in the spare room. Unable to settle, Blizzard drove instead to Abbey Road, allowing his thoughts to roam as he guided the car along the dark country lanes between his village and the orange glow of the city. They were still turbulent as he pulled into the half-empty car park of the police station, a selection of prefabs supposed to be temporary but still there thirty years later. Few officers were on duty and the chief inspector had enjoyed the solitude as he walked along the dimly-lit corridors towards his office.

Having sat for the best part of an hour, he had still failed to come up with a rational explanation for what had happened the previous evening. And not for the first time. He knew the girl was Pauline Galston but also that she was not real. He did not believe in ghosts. It could not go on, he knew that, and despite his longstanding suspicion of the medical profession, Blizzard reluctantly resolved to go back to his GP. The chief inspector flicked on the reading lamp and tried to concentrate on the pile of reports in front of him. But, having scanned the same line half a dozen times without taking it in, he tossed the file back onto his cluttered desk.

'Bloody HR,' he grunted. 'Haven't they got anything better to do with their sodding time?'

He sat in silence for a moment or two, staring moodily out of the window into the rain-flecked darkness again, and inevitably his thoughts turned to Danny Galston. What was required, Blizzard had asserted on being appointed head of Western Division's DCI, was a cold-case review and a dedicated team to follow it through. However, every time he thought he had freed up a couple of officers, something happened to derail his plans. Blizzard scowled at the documents on his desk: if it wasn't crime, it was paperwork. It was no wonder he never got round to locking up Danny Galston.

But he knew there was more to it than that: headquarters viewed the Galston case as unsolvable. Privately, and in his more irrational moments, the chief inspector wondered if the fact that Danny Galston had been a police officer in one of the constabulary's rural divisions, before coming to Hafton to start his haulage company, was anything to do with it. He remembered a weary Harry Roberts sitting in this very same office at Abbey Road one night three months after the killings, cradling a glass of whisky and turning hooded eyes on his colleague as he said in a quiet voice: 'There are too many secrets here, Johnny, my boy.' He had refused to elaborate and 15 years later, the words still had a troubling resonance.

There was a light knock on the door and in walked Colley. As the sergeant slumped on a chair, careful not to spill any of tea from the mug he was carrying, the chief inspector eyed him affectionately. Blizzard did not like many people, but he liked David Colley. The sergeant was everything his boss was not. Affable and easy-going, he was a decade younger and much sharper in appearance. Tall and lean, a result of his rugby playing, the detective sergeant had black hair which was neatly combed as always; his round, almost boyish, face was clean-shaven; his black trousers, blue shirt and grey jacket were all perfectly ironed by Jay; and his black shoes gleamed.

'In early,' said Blizzard, looking at his weary sergeant.

'Jay had a crappy night so I've let her sleep in.'

'What about work?'

'Not sure she could face the little darlings this morning. I'll ring the headteacher later.'

'She missed a couple of days last week as well, didn't she?'

'Yeah.'

'She ill then?'

'Er, no. That is, yes. Well, sort of.'

Blizzard raised an eyebrow.

'A bug,' said Colley.

'Ah,' said Blizzard, giving the merest of smiles. 'And do you think you'll come down with it?'

'I can safely say I won't. Anyway, what is this, twenty bloody questions?'

'Sorry,' replied Blizzard.

'No, I'm sorry. Just a bit tired, that's all,' said the sergeant. Eager to change the subject, he looked closely at his colleague. 'Last night in the cemetery. What did you see?'

'Nothing.'

'But you said...'

'Leave it.'

There was an uncomfortable silence after which the sergeant got up and walked out into the corridor, watched with consternation by his boss. The last thing Blizzard wanted to do was offend his trusted right-hand man.

'Where you going?' shouted Blizzard.

'To start again,' said the sergeant's disembodied voice from the corridor. 'I'll be David Colley, you can be John Blizzard. You need to remember he's a grumpy old bastard. Ready?'

'Yeah, ready,' chuckled Blizzard, relieved that the sergeant's customary good humour had resurfaced.

There was a knock on the door and in walked Colley.

'Good morning, guv,' he said.

'Good morning, David,' said Blizzard.

Both men grinned; it was a ridiculous little charade but it banished the tension from the room.

'I did some checking,' said Colley, lowering himself back into the seat and reaching out to the desk for his tea. 'The Galston gravestone was not the only one attacked with paint. There have been others in recent weeks. Uniform reckon it's kids.'

'I am sure they do.'

'You don't sound convinced.'

'I'm not sure what I think,' said Blizzard, wincing as he shifted in his seat.

'Pills not doing any good then?'

The chief inspector shook his head and grimaced as the pain stabbed again at his back. The spasms had come on several weeks previously after he spent two hours in driving rain, watching officers searching derelict docklands for clothes linked to a murder inquiry. Reluctantly, the chief inspector had gone to see his GP three days later when the pain became too severe and he was forced to spend two days in bed. The doctor had diagnosed mild fibrositis, cheerfully told him his spine was crumbling and prescribed painkillers and rest. Faced with a growing caseload, Blizzard took the pills but ignored his recommendation to take it easy and had returned to work the following day, although he was still moving with some difficulty three weeks later.

'Perhaps you should have a few days off, guv. Fee reckons you are overdoing…'

'Yes, thank you,' said the chief inspector. His voice was one of resignation rather than annoyance. 'However, when I need health advice from you I'll let you know. And you can stop grinning like the sodding Cheshire cat. Why don't you do something useful?'

'I'll do some more checking with the cemetery people. Meanwhile, are we going to do anything about Danny Galston?'

'Like what?'

'You said you were going to talk to the CPS again.'

'And much good did it do me. They haven't budged an inch; without new evidence we can't pull him in. They're still terrified that his lawyer will slap an injunction on us if I so much as fart in Danny's street.'

'I'm not surprised the CPS are worried,' said Colley, his mind going back to an unpleasant confrontation with Galston's solicitor two years earlier. 'He certainly goes to great lengths to stay away from us.'

'Yeah, he does and I really cannot see a way round it, I am afraid.'

'We could always check if the tax disc on his lorry is out of date. What you laughing at? You're always telling us to be more inventive.'

'So I am. Hey, it may not be as stupid as it sounds.'

'It was only a joke.'

'I know but the CPS only said we could not interview Danny about the murders. What if we went to see him about something else?'

'You surely don't mean the tax...?'

'No, the bloody vandalism! After all, we are investigating it, aren't we?'

'We are now.'

* * *

Half an hour later, having driven to the city's leafy west end, the officers parked in Laurel Avenue, pushed open an ornate front gate set in a large perimeter wall and walked up the gravelled drive to Danny Galston's detached mock-Georgian house, outside which were parked a red Jaguar and a large, mud-spattered truck. The officers were conscious of being watched balefully from the front window by a wiry man in his mid-forties, his hair short, dark and greasy and his face bearing faint traces of childhood acne. The man, who was wearing blue work overalls, suddenly dipped out of sight and moments later wrenched open the front door to stand pointing at them, his hand trembling with fury.

'I told you I don't want to talk to you coppers,' he shouted. 'Sod off!'

'See,' said the chief inspector, glancing at his sergeant, 'Danny never did lose his affection for the job.'

'My lawyer told you to keep away and if you don't get off my property in the next ten seconds, I'll kick you off myself!'

'I'm sure you will,' said Blizzard, glancing at Galston's scuffed work boots. 'But it's hardly the way to talk to people trying to help you, is it?'

'You ain't never helped me! This is harassment and I will tell my…'

'Keep your hat on, Danny,' said Blizzard. 'We're not here to talk about the murders.'

'So, what you here for then?'

'We're investigating the vandalism at the grave.'

'What vandalism?' said Galston, calming down slightly.

'You mean you didn't know?'

Galston shook his head, the rage leaving him as suddenly as it had arrived.

'You'd better come in,' he said, standing aside to let them through.

He led them down a spacious hallway adorned by a large gold-framed mirror, and into an expansive living room carpeted in plush blue and furnished with a black leather sofa. A couple of original paintings of seafaring scenes hung on the wall, all thunderous skies and raging waves, and a large antique vase stood on the sideboard. The back window of the knock-through room looked out over a long garden complete with summer house and a couple of elegant statues depicting half-naked Roman women bearing fruit. They looked expensive, thought Blizzard. In fact, everything looked expensive: the haulage business had certainly been good to Danny Galston.

The chief inspector stood by the mantlepiece and glanced down at the colour photograph by his arm, a wedding picture taken in the sun-drenched garden of a local country house hotel, showing a beaming Galston wearing a dark suit and holding the hand of a stunning blonde a decade younger than himself. This was Cara, whom the haulier had married five years after the murders. As ever, two things struck the chief inspector about the image: how could such an attractive young woman hook up with a scumbag like Danny Galston, and where were the pictures of Jenny and the kids?

'Cara OK?' asked the chief inspector.

'What vandalism?' said Galston, ignoring the question.

'Someone threw red paint,' said Colley. 'I really am surprised you didn't know about it. I mean, yesterday was the anniversary, wasn't it?'

'I didn't go,' said Galston, walking over to stare moodily out of the front window.

'But surely on such a special day...'

'It's not what you think,' said Galston sharply, turning and glaring at the sergeant. 'Gerry Brauner would have been waiting for me to turn up. He's been after me again.'

Colley, who had experienced his own run-ins with the freelance photographer down the years, nodded. It explained a lot.

'You have my sympathies,' he said. 'What did he want, as if I didn't know?'

'The usual. A picture of me placing flowers at the grave. Reckons the nationals will pay good money for it. Fifteenth anniversary, see. He's been making my life a misery, ringing at all hours, shoving notes through the door, hassling people I know. Even offering them money. He's the one you should be after.'

'Why not just let him do it?' asked Blizzard. 'He'll stop then, surely.'

'His kind never stop. Besides,' Galston laughed bitterly, 'the papers would love that. You saw what they wrote when it happened. Practically called me a murderer. I should have sued the lot of them. Is the gravestone badly damaged?'

'It'll clean up,' said Blizzard. 'Any idea who would want to damage it?'

'Take your pick.' Galston gave another mirthless laugh. 'There's plenty of people think I killed them, including you lot. But I didn't.'

For a moment the officers detected sadness behind the eyes and neither of them felt inclined to dispute his statement; it did not seem the time. Besides, there was always his lawyer to think about.

'Yes, well we're not here to talk about the murders, Danny,' said Blizzard. 'You see, when we saw the vandalism, we thought…'

'I know what you thought and I'm not going to fall for it,' said Galston. He glanced at his watch. 'I'm late for a job. Any more stupid questions?'

Blizzard shook his head and walked into the hall; he had only wanted to remind Galston that he had not forgotten about the killings. It might be a crude tactic but the chief inspector felt better for having employed it.

'Well, thank you for your time, Danny,' said Blizzard as Galston opened the door.

'Good day, gentlemen,' said Galston coldly.

The detectives stepped outside.

'Hang on a minute,' said Colley, peering at the truck parked nearby. 'Isn't that tax disc out of date, Danny?'

Galston slammed the door in their faces.

Chapter three

Shortly before eight the next morning, Blizzard and Colley were sitting in the chief inspector's office, enjoying mugs of tea before Western Division came calling once more. She always did. She was a demanding mistress. The city's largest patch, the division stretched from the rural flatlands and leafy avenues of Hafton's affluent western outskirts, through the semi-detached neighbourhoods surrounding Abbey Road Police Station, on to a darker world of crumbling blocks of flats, neglected maisonettes and run-down council houses – sprawling areas littered with burnt-out cars, used syringes, and abandoned pushchairs. Heading further towards the city centre, there was the seething cesspit of bedsit-land in once-proud Victorian terraces and, sloping down to the banks of the murky River Haft, the expanse of derelict shipyards and docklands with their red-light areas.

With the division experiencing a high crime rate, any snatched moments of respite were greatly appreciated by its officers and neither Blizzard or Colley felt particularly minded to start their working day as they sat in comfortable silence. The day ahead for Colley meant an ongoing inquiry into a series of burglaries on one of the housing estates, an investigation in which he was close to an arrest. For his part, the chief inspector, who was sitting with his feet up on the desk after discovering some days earlier that the pose alleviated his back problems, had cleared his diary to review progress on a robbery inquiry. From time to time, in between gulps of tea, he slid guilty looks at the reports piled up in his in-tray.

Out in the corridor, the detectives could hear the sounds of the police station waking up, doors opening and shutting, office lights clicking on and the cheery greetings of people at the vending machine. In the cosiness of the office, with the rain driving against the window, they seemed a world away and Colley, having endured another difficult night as Jay struggled with the effects of pregnancy, found himself starting to nod off over the rugby reports he was reading in the newspaper.

'You look tired,' said Blizzard.

'Jay's still unwell.'

'Nasty bug.'

'You could always give me the day off.'

'I'd rather have Billy Jacobs lifted for those burglaries. HQ's been on about detection rates again.'

'Thought you'd say that,' said the sergeant gloomily.

'I suppose we ought to make a move then,' said the chief inspector, swinging his legs on to the floor and wincing at the pain. 'However, we have some important top-level stuff to do first. Come on.'

'Where we going?'

'Lil's. One of her bacon butties will do us the world of good. An army marches on a full stomach.'

'Yours certainly does,' said Colley, glancing at Blizzard's paunch as the chief inspector struggled into his jacket.

'Yes, thank you, Sergeant,' said Blizzard.

'Anyway, I thought Fee said you shouldn't eat too much fat.'

'She's on a day off...'

'Lucky basket.'

'And what she can't see, can't harm her,' said the chief inspector. He headed for the door. 'Besides, I've had enough sodding broccoli pancakes to last me a lifetime. Have you ever eaten odour-eaters?'

'Can't say I have.'

'Well, I imagine they taste the same as broccoli pancakes. Are you coming or what?'

'Too bloody right,' said the sergeant.

He slipped his newspaper into his suit jacket pocket and stood up. A uniformed officer popped her head round the door.

'Sorry to interrupt you, sir,' she said, looking at Blizzard, 'but Control have just been on. There's been a body found at Hafton Cemetery.'

'There's a joke in there somewhere,' said Colley.

But Blizzard was already on his way out of the office.

* * *

Half an hour later, having battled through morning rush-hour traffic, the detectives were standing once more at the Galston grave, surrounded by trees dripping with the rain that had been falling for several minutes. Stretched out before them, blood oozing from an ugly wound to the back of his head, blue overalls smeared with mud and hand still clutching a bunch of flowers, lay the dead man.

'So, does this count as new evidence?' asked Colley flatly.

'Even if it did, I somehow doubt you'd be able to interview him,' said Blizzard grimly. 'Whatever he knew, Danny Galston has taken it with him.'

The chief inspector crouched down and reached out a hand to touch the flowers, the bright yellow blooms splashed with blood; it reminded him of the paint thrown across the gravestone the previous day and still there now. Blizzard stared at the flowers, suddenly struck by the realisation that they were the symbol of a man who cared, a man who had come to mourn his wife and young child.

A man who had come to pay his respects and who now lay beside them in death. Blizzard glanced up at the overcast sky.

'He's all yours now, Harry,' he murmured.

'Guv?' asked Colley.

'Nothing,' said the chief inspector. He looked back at the body. 'Damn!'

He stood up and looked over to one of the uniformed officers standing nearby.

'Who found him, Don?'

'The cemetery manager.' The officer nodded towards a man leaning against a gravestone along one of the nearby paths. 'Lives in that house by the entrance. Desmond Roach is his name.'

Blizzard surveyed the manager, who was trembling slightly and staring hard at the ground. Wearing a grubby Parka over ill-fitting brown cords and a green shirt, Roach was in his late twenties, had short greasy black hair, gaunt features and dark eyes which gave him a funereal appearance. Just the kind of man to work in a cemetery, thought Blizzard.

'Remind me not to die,' he muttered.

Colley gave a low laugh then wiped the smile from his face: the sound had seemed to echo round the cemetery and Colley sensed that he had disturbed the sanctity of the place.

'Sorry,' he said.

Blizzard nodded then looked once more at Desmond Roach.

'What do you make of him, Don?' he asked.

'Something funny there.'

'He doesn't look like he does funny. What do you mean?'

'He looks nervous.'

'So would you be if you'd just found a body.'

'It's more than that, John. There's a rabbit away, you mark my words.'

'Well, let's find out,' said Blizzard, walking over to the cemetery manager. 'Mr Roach, I wonder if you could answer a few questions?'

'Like what?'

Blizzard smiled thinly; something in the slightly whining tone irritated him and he liked dealing with people who irritated him, it always made it easier to turn on the pressure if required.

'Like, for a start, the sign at the entrance says you do not open the gates until 9am but this fellow was already here. Someone must have let him in. Was that you?'

'I ain't done nothing wrong.'

'No one said you had but it's a simple enough question and I would appreciate an answer.'

'I don't know what you are talking about,' said Roach. 'All I know is…'

'You seem to be rather flush this morning,' interrupted Colley.

Roach watched uneasily as Colley reached down to pick up a bundle of bank notes that had fallen from the manager's trouser pocket.

'Two hundred quid,' said the sergeant with a low whistle. 'Care to tell me where it came from?'

'It was given to me.'

'What generous friends you have, Mr Roach,' said Blizzard drily.

'I didn't nick it, if that's what you're thinking. Danny gave it to me.'

'Yeah, why wait for the will, eh?' said Blizzard.

'I didn't steal it from him! Me and Danny was friends. He's been coming ever since I've worked here. Never misses an anniversary.'

'But the anniversary was two days ago,' said Colley.

'There's this photographer, bloke called Gerry Brauner. Comes along every anniversary. Pretends to be putting flowers on a grave but he's here for hours. Doesn't know I've clocked him but I have.' Roach sounded proud.

'So Danny comes in a couple of days late to throw Brauner off the scent?' asked Blizzard.

'Yeah. He slips me £200 and I open the gates early for him. We done the same thing every year.'

'When did you let him in this morning?'

'Seven-fifteen.'

'And how come it was you who found his body?' asked the chief inspector.

'I ain't done nothing wrong.'

'So you keep telling us,' said Blizzard. 'Although I am beginning to wonder.'

'We just want to know how you found the body,' said Colley. 'That's all, Desmond. Come on, out with it.'

Roach looked at the sergeant's encouraging expression and nodded.

'I was walking the dog,' he said, gesturing to a miserable terrier-like creature tied to one of the trees and shivering in the chill drizzle.

'Is that what it is?' scowled Blizzard, who detested pets of any description. 'I take it Danny Galston was dead when your rat found him?'

Roach looked as if he was about to remonstrate but one glance at the chief inspector's expression changed his mind.

'Yeah,' said Roach. 'I was terrified. I thought you might reckon I done it.'

'The thought had occurred,' murmured the chief inspector.

'Well, I didn't! I liked Danny Galston. He was always good to me – and he never missed an anniversary.'

'What, never?' said the chief inspector.

'Na, never. He was real upset every time he came here.'

Blizzard said nothing.

'Did you let anyone else into the cemetery early this morning?' asked Colley.

'Like who?'

The manager's reply seemed just a touch too quick.

'You do seem nervous, Mr Roach,' said Blizzard.

'I ain't supposed to let anyone in early, it's against the rules. If they find out, I'll get sacked. You won't tell them, will you?'

'We won't need to,' said Blizzard. 'The media will be all over this like a rash. It won't take your bosses long to work out your little game.'

Roach looked at him miserably.

'Tell me,' said the chief inspector, glancing back at the body, 'did Danny ever mention Pauline?'

'Na, not really. He showed me a photograph of her once and she looked a bit, well, strange, like.'

'Yes,' murmured Blizzard, 'I imagine she did.'

The chief inspector left Colley to conclude the questioning and walked across the grass. He scanned the deserted cemetery and his thoughts came back to Roach's comments about Danny Galston's love for his young family. For the first time in fifteen years, the chief inspector realised he may have to confront some difficult questions. Blizzard turned when he heard Colley walking towards him.

'Perhaps Danny was a victim as well,' said the sergeant, echoing the chief inspector's thoughts.

'He is now.'

'Still not telling me what spooked you?'

'No.'

'Why the secrecy?'

'I didn't see anything and that's all there is to it.'

'But…'

'But nothing!'

Colley shrugged and walked away. Blizzard resumed his perusal of the cemetery, half expecting to see the strange little girl standing in the shadows again. But he saw no one and the dead slept on. And this time, Danny Galston slept with them.

Chapter four

Cara Galston did a good grieving widow. It probably came
from her days in amateur dramatics when she was much
younger, she reflected as she stood at the living room
window that afternoon, watching the last of the well-
wishers walk down the drive. Georgia Horwood, her
closest confidante for many years, had been with her for
several hours, and as her friend neared the wrought-iron
gate, Cara's mind drifted back to when they had appeared
in that performance on stage together. Shakespeare was a
bit high-brow for the dead-beats of Hafton Amateur
Dramatic Society, Cara had thought at the time, but the
producer was desperate to make a name for himself with
something more challenging than Brian Rix farces. Cara
found it easy to persuade the earnest young man to give
her a leading role. She liked being the centre of attention
and all it took was a few well-aimed remarks about his
artistic vision and the part was hers – even before she slept
with him to make sure.

Georgia had only been given a bit-part but Cara's
hard-earned role had given her the opportunity to shine.
Oh, how the audience had stood and applauded at the end.
Cara remembered the last night when someone even threw

a bunch of roses onto the stage at Hafton Civic Theatre. Attractive young man, he was. Funny how good things always happened to her in November, she mused as she waved when Georgia turned at the front gate for one last look. Cara suddenly felt tired; she had been acting all day as a succession of friends came to comfort her after Danny's death and it had proved a strain. The performance had started when she pretended to be devastated as Blizzard and Colley sat in her living room and told her the news. She had staggered slightly – a nice touch, she thought – and allowed the sergeant to guide her gently to a chair then bring her a cup of water.

Giving herself time to recover, and enjoying the attention of the good-looking officer, Cara had passed a hand across her brow – not too dramatic, didn't want to overplay it – then turned moist eyes on the detectives. Deliberately allowing the tears to flow more freely as Blizzard tried to ask her some questions, she contemplated passing out for a moment or two to shut him up but opted instead for feeling faint and they had left, promising to come back later.

* * *

Walking across the living room towards the kitchen, Cara stopped and admired herself in the full-length mirror hanging to one side of the sideboard. Not bad for thirty-seven, she told herself, admiring her curves. She knew she was still attractive, her hair bottle blonde, her complexion blemish-free and her eyes displaying no signs of tell-tale crow's feet; Cara Galston had done everything in her power to stay the sands of time. Today, she was dressed casually in white trainers, grey designer tracksuit trousers and a tight pale blue T-shirt that showed off her tight stomach, the result of many hours in the gym, and breasts surgically enhanced the year before. Cara gave a satisfied nod; yes, not bad, not bad at all, my girl.

She frowned, recalling again the conversation with the detectives that morning. The sergeant had been alright but something about Blizzard's demeanour as he sat on the sofa, eying her intently having told her that her husband was dead, had troubled Cara. She remembered – kept coming back to it time and time again – how Georgia's emotional intervention had come at just the right time because, good actress or not, Cara Galston had found it difficult to conceal her irritation at the chief inspector's questions. Danny had never trusted him either. The haulier had told his wife several times that the chief inspector was convinced he murdered his first wife and the two children. Cara had never asked if he had. Suddenly, though, the darkness was banished and she smiled again as she recalled David Colley; it had been down to the nice sergeant to provide the sympathy. Was the sergeant married, she wondered as she switched on the kettle then stood staring out of the kitchen window at the garden, the sun glinting off the Romanesque statues. She struggled to recall if the sergeant had worn a ring. She was sure he hadn't.

Her mind wandered back to Danny. It was always his wealth that had attracted her. Cara's first marriage had been a disaster, leaving her to pay off her feckless ex-husband's debts, so she was desperate for money. She knew from the beginning that it was a bad marriage, of course – the shadows of his dead family seemed always to hang over them – but she ignored it as best she could. His money was ample compensation.

As Cara stood in her hand-crafted kitchen, her eyes ranged over the huge fridge-freezer specially imported from the US, the glass-fronted cabinets containing tastefully backlit ornaments, the shelves containing the antique jugs that had cost her a small fortune and the wine rack containing only the best. Oh, yes, she thought as her mind went back to those sour-faced women at the haulage association dinners Danny dragged her to, she had what they didn't, alright.

Besides, Cara told herself as she opened one of her cupboards and took out a box of chamomile tea, had she not enjoyed her little dalliances down the years, her little forays into other men's beds when Danny was out in his truck?

Well, she thought as the kettle boiled, she would not need to do any skulking in the shadows now. Danny Galston was dead and his poor grieving widow had inherited his share of the business. By her reckoning – and she had been reckoning it for a long while – she was now worth the thick end of £10m. Much more if everything went to plan.

Cara hesitated, teabag hovering over the antique china teapot; had she felt anything when she heard that Danny was dead? Had she experienced a tug of... a tug of what exactly? Guilt, she supposed, but only for a second or two. Yes, something had gone from her life and perhaps, in a way, it was sad. But not that sad. Not ten million-quidsworth sad. This was no time to entertain doubts. Cara looked out over the garden again. November always had been a lucky month for her. A broad smile transformed her face and this time, she was not acting.

Chapter five

Old friends John Blizzard and his boss, Detective Superintendent Arthur Ronald, sat drinking mugs of tea at Abbey Road. As darkness fell outside and rain started to lash the window of Ronald's office once again, Blizzard updated him on the inquiry, announcing to the superintendent's consternation that he was convinced Cara Galston was faking grief. The chief inspector, Ronald noted gloomily, seemed to be enjoying himself, tilting back on his chair with a satisfied, almost mischievous expression on his face. For the superintendent's part, he was too busy running through the ramifications of arresting a grieving widow in full glare of the media less than 24 hours after her husband's high-profile murder to take much notice. As usual, the chief inspector was much less mindful of such sensitivities. Assuming he was mindful of them at all, which Ronald very much doubted.

Despite their close relationship, they were contrasting characters. Ronald, married with two teenaged children, was a pudgy, balding man with ruddy cheeks and eyes with bags which sagged darkly. A man given to constant worrying about mortgages and university fees, he was not yet fifty but looked older. A smart dresser with shoes that always shined, a sharply-pressed suit and tie constantly done up, he masked his sharp edges with an avuncular façade and consummate political skills. None of which applied to John Blizzard, who masked nothing and whose devilish tendency to suggest the controversial had surfaced yet again as he warmed to his theme.

'So, what I reckon is...' continued Blizzard.

'Yes, yes,' said Ronald irritably, 'but I've already said you can't arrest Cara Galston without evidence.'

'Might shake her up a bit.'

'She's just lost her husband! How shaken up do you want her to be, for Christ's sake?'

Blizzard shrugged. 'It's just a thought.'

Ronald sighed. He knew all about John Blizzard's thoughts and he knew that, more often than not, they were right. Having first worked with Ronald when they were rookies, Blizzard had been the superintendent's first appointment when, four years previously, he assumed command of CID in the force's southern half, which included the city of Hafton. There had been those, the chief constable among them, who doubted the wisdom of such a decision, concerned by Blizzard's somewhat maverick tendencies. However, subsequent events vindicated Ronald's judgement as the division's rocketing crime rate slowed, then halted and was now tumbling as detection rates went up. But Ronald had long since realised that, if he wanted the benefits of working with John Blizzard, he also had to live with some of the disadvantages. The superintendent tried again.

'From my point of view...' he began.

'Something's wrong, Arthur, I can feel it in my water,' said Blizzard earnestly, then held up his hands at Ronald's expression. 'OK, OK, I know, I need something more for the CPS.'

'Too right. The CPS has never placed much credence on your urine.'

'If you ask me, they've been taking the p...'

'Yes, thank you,' said Ronald wearily. 'So, have you got any evidence?'

'Well, not in the conventional sense but something will turn up. It always does.'

'Yes, well until it does...' Ronald left the sentence unfinished.

Blizzard frowned. He knew Ronald was right but it did not change his conviction that Cara Galston had been playing a part that morning. Ever since the detectives had left the house, all Blizzard could think about was the way she had taken the news. Right words, yes, right gestures, yes, but wrong body language. He could not shrug off the feeling that she was playing a part for the detectives' benefit. However, Blizzard knew he was alone in his suspicions; Colley certainly did not believe him. All the sergeant had seen was a grieving widow. It was tragic, Colley had said, that such an attractive woman should be left alone. Blizzard had given him a withering look but knew he could not compete with the widow's pert breasts.

'It's just...' the chief inspector began again.

'What about that photographer bloke Gerry Brauner?' asked Ronald, cutting across him. 'His grubby mitts seem to be all over this one.'

* * *

In fact, as they were speaking, Colley and the cemetery manager, Desmond Roach, were discussing Gerry Brauner as they sat in one of the interview rooms at the other end of the police station. Roach had walked into the reception a quarter of an hour earlier and demanded to see the sergeant. He stared across the table with a hunted look in his eyes.

'I ain't been totally straight with you, Mr Colley,' said Roach.

'Now there's a bombshell, Desmond.'

'I asked for you 'cause I don't reckon Mr Blizzard would understand.'

'I imagine you are right,' said Colley. 'So, what brings you here?'

'Gerry Brauner, he told me to say nothing but I can't sit on this,' said Roach, speaking quickly as if relieved to finally unburden himself. 'It's doing my head in. Brauner were at the cemetery this morning at the same time Danny got killed. I know that because I let him in.'

'And why, pray, why did you do that? And how come Brauner knew that Danny Galston would be there?'

'He slipped me £50 to let him know the arrangements,' said Roach, looking ever more uncomfortable. 'Said he would double it if he got a good picture.'

'That's two hundred from Danny Galston and fifty from Brauner. You seem to be making a healthy profit out of all this death business,' said Colley. 'Do you know if our friend Mr Brauner got a good picture?'

'Dunno.'

'Did you see him afterwards?'

'Only when I opened the gate to let him out. Then, when I took the dog for a walk, I found the body.'

* * *

Ten minutes later, Blizzard and the superintendent were still deep in conversation when the sergeant arrived at the office.

'Anything?' asked Ronald, relieved at the distraction.

'He off on one?' grinned Colley, nodding at the chief inspector.

'You could say that. Wants the widow Galston stringing up.'

'Not an entirely unattractive thought,' said Colley. 'She is a bit of a looker and I am pretty sure that her br...'

'Yes, thank you, Sergeant,' said Ronald. 'Apart from your sordid fantasies, have you found out anything interesting?'

'Desmond Roach says Brauner was there when Galston was murdered. And no, Desmond did not see the widow Galston bashing her husband's brains out with a stone angel.'

'Yes, thank you, Sergeant,' said Blizzard.

'What's more, Gerry Brauner has an interesting line in pastimes,' said Colley, fishing a piece of paper out of his jacket pocket. 'Uniform say that a week or so ago, they received a complaint about him pestering Ralph Cargill.'

'That's Galston's business partner, isn't it?' said Ronald.

'Yeah. The complaint related to a big bust-up outside the depot. Cargill told uniform that Brauner was harassing him, Brauner said Cargill smashed his camera.'

'I think our Mr Brauner is definitely worth talking to,' said Ronald, looking pointedly at the chief inspector.

'Too right,' said Colley. 'If you ask me, guv, Dessy Boy and Snapper-Man are up to their neck in the brown stuff on this one.'

'I assume there is an English translation for that?' asked Ronald, looking at Blizzard.

'I'll get you a phrase book for Christmas,' said Blizzard. 'Come on, Sergeant, time we paid our Mr Brauner a visit, I think.'

* * *

Halfway through a telephone conversation shortly after six-thirty, Gerry Brauner glanced out of his first-floor office window and noticed the two detectives walking towards the building. Sitting at his untidy desk, he sighed as he watched the officers pick their way between the parked cars that always thronged the dimly-lit city centre back street, even during the evening. Not that the officers' appearance was a surprise; the death of Danny Galston had put him centre stage in their inquiry and he knew it. So did the man at the other end of the telephone receiver.

'Gerry, are you there?' asked the man.

'Yeah, but I gotta go. Inspector Knacker's here.'

'Who is it?'

'Blizzard and that sergeant of his. Colley.'

'Yeah, well just remember what I said, keep your trap shut.'

'Don't worry, I can handle them.'

'Make sure you do,' said the man and the line went dead.

Brauner scowled and replaced the receiver. Up until then, he had been enjoying a good day. One of his best. The kind of day to kill for, he had told himself on several occasions, laughing as he did so. Desmond Roach had rung him about the body early that morning and by 10am, Brauner had already been twice warned off by police as he tried to sneak into Hafton Cemetery – once as he was squeezing through a gap in the hedge along the main road, the second time as he was scaling the perimeter wall. It was only when a burly uniformed sergeant threatened to confiscate his camera that Brauner retreated. Not that he went far: a body in a cemetery was already a good enough story but instinct told him there was more to it than that.

He was right. Early in the afternoon, in response to intense media pressure, the force confirmed that the corpse was Danny Galston and, since then, Brauner's phone had been ringing constantly with national newspapers demanding pictures. They all knew Brauner was the man to come to because he had taken plenty of shots of Galston down the years. Besides, he had the image everyone was after. Name your price, the nationals had said, and Brauner had done just that, spending several hours with a broad grin on his face as he wired his pictures. He even sold some images to a couple of foreign newspapers. Oh, how he loved a feeding frenzy! That fifty quid he had slipped Desmond Roach for the heads-up on Galston's plans was the best money he'd spent in a long time.

Just before Blizzard and Colley appeared on the street, Brauner had been sitting at his litter-strewn desk, gulping tea from a cracked green mug, eating a ham sandwich and jotting down how much he had earned that day. He had just reckoned it must run into five figures and was contemplating popping into the Red Lion, the shabby pub on the ground floor, for a celebratory drink when the telephone rang. The freelance photographer knew it was the man. He knew the man would be panicking. The phone call confirmed it; Brauner could sense the fear in the man's voice when he heard that the police had come calling.

Brauner wasn't worried, however; now approaching forty, he was well used to dealing with awkward police officers, even the notoriously difficult John Blizzard. A freelance photographer for the best part of a decade, specialising in seedy foot-in-the-door exclusives for the tabloids, he was doing very well for himself even though his appearance – overweight, black hair greasy and unkempt and leather jacket worn at the elbows – might suggest down-at-heel. It was a carefully cultivated image because that was the kind of world Brauner moved in. On hearing a sharp banging on the side door downstairs, he sighed, hauled himself out of his ramshackle chair and picked his way slowly down the narrow, dark stairway.

'Well, this is a lovely surprise,' he said as he opened the door.

'Yeah, I'm sure,' grunted Blizzard. 'Time for a chat?'

'Well, actually I was going to give the office a hoover so perhaps you could come back later.'

'I think not,' said Blizzard.

The detectives pushed their way into the building and clattered up the stairs into the office.

'Business not very good then, Gerry?' said Blizzard. He surveyed the single light bulb, rusting filing cabinet and bare, damp-stained walls. 'This place is a shit hole.'

'I work here because it's cheap. Besides, image isn't everything. You should know that.'

Blizzard ignored the comment.

'So,' said Brauner returning to his chair behind the desk, the only one in the room. 'What do you want?'

'Danny Galston.'

'He ain't here.'

'Don't play clever with me!' snapped Blizzard. 'He's dead and I want to know if you had anything to do with it.'

'I just take photographs.'

'You do a damned sight more than that. You've been harassing him.'

'I prefer to describe it as nurturing a contact.'

'And we know you were trying to get pictures of him at the grave,' said Blizzard.

He wandered over to the window and watched a couple of drunken men lurching their way towards the Red Lion.

'So?' said Brauner.

'So maybe Danny told you to sling your hook,' said Blizzard, talking in a deliberately distracted way as he watched the drunks. 'Maybe you grabbed the first thing at hand and hit him.'

'Na, you got it wrong. I wasn't even there when he was killed.'

'We'll know soon enough, won't we?' said Blizzard. He walked over to the desk. 'If you did get a shot at the grave, it'll be all over the papers, will it not?'

'OK, OK, so I got a pic. But that's all that happened.'

'You expect us to believe that? I mean, look at it from our point of view, Gerry. You turn up and lo and behold, look what happens – poor old Danny Galston gets killed. Whoops.'

'Now hang on, Blizzard,' protested Brauner. 'All I did was hide behind a tree and get my shot of him dumping the flowers with a long lens.'

'Such a noble profession,' murmured Blizzard.

'I never killed him. Honest.'

'Now there is a word you wouldn't expect to hear a journalist use,' said the chief inspector. He gestured towards the door. 'Shall we?'

And the detectives led Brauner out of his office.

Chapter six

'This does not look good,' said Blizzard, tossing The Sun onto the interview room desk the next morning. 'It really does not.'

'Actually, it looks very good,' replied Brauner.

He viewed with satisfaction the front page, which was dominated by a large colour image of Danny Galston sprawled by the gravestone. *A killer's final farewell,* said the headline.

'A few thousand quid's worth of good, to be precise,' added Brauner. 'Any of the others gone with it on the front page?'

'The Star and the Mirror as well,' said Colley, who was sitting at the table.

'Excellent,' said Brauner, glancing at his lawyer, a sallow besuited man in his fifties. 'It'll pay your extortionate fees anyway, Richard.'

'Start talking seriously about this, will you?' exclaimed Blizzard, sitting down next to his sergeant and stabbing the paper with a finger. 'Danny Galston gets his head stoved in and you are there taking his sodding picture – what the hell is that supposed to make us think, Gerry?'

'I believe,' said Richard Burns, in a slightly nasal voice, 'that my client has made it abundantly clear that all he wanted was a picture. It may be somewhat distasteful but the last time I checked, it was not against the law.'

'It is if you kill him to get it.'

'I really do think this has gone far enough,' said the lawyer. 'Are you sure this is not really about your well-known dislike of journalists?'

Blizzard said nothing; he realised that becoming involved in a slanging match with the solicitor would achieve little.

'So,' continued Burns, 'unless you have some evidence to link my client to this murder, I feel that this interview is at an end.'

'What did you want with Ralph Cargill?' asked Colley, looking at Brauner. 'I can understand why you were hassling Galston but where does his business partner come into it?'

'It's nothing.'

'Sounded liked a lot for nothing,' said the sergeant. 'According to uniform, it got quite nasty.'

'OK, OK. I offered Cargill a few quid if he would persuade Danny to go for a picture by the grave.'

'And?'

'He went ballistic, called me some names, grabbed my camera bag. One of the lenses got smashed. It was no big deal.'

'Maybe the same thing happened when Danny saw you in the cemetery yesterday morning,' said Blizzard. 'Maybe things got out of hand then as well.'

Before Brauner could reply, there was a knock at the door and the chief inspector made his excuses and walked out into the corridor. He was met by Detective Inspector Graham Ross, divisional head of forensics at Abbey Road, dressed immaculately as ever, in a pressed grey designer suit with red silk tie and expensive, shiny black shoes.

Blizzard, crumpled as usual, viewed the DI's attire with his customary sour look.

'This had better be good, Versace,' grunted Blizzard, 'because at the moment we have nothing against this guy.'

'Sorry to disappoint, guv, but there's nothing to suggest he attacked chummy.'

'For God's sake, he was hiding behind a tree taking his bleeding picture!' exclaimed Blizzard. 'How much more do you need?'

'A lot more, I am afraid. One of our lads has looked at the pictures Brauner wired to the papers and they were definitely taken with a long lens. He was probably twenty or thirty metres away. We can't find any that suggestion that he got any nearer.'

'Marvellous,' said Blizzard, turning to walk back into the interview room. 'Bloody marvellous.'

* * *

Twenty minutes later, Gerry Brauner walked out into the bright winter sunlight, a broad grin all over his face; he had some invoices to write. The chief inspector, for his part, headed back to his office and sat in moody silence for a few minutes, turning over the interview in his mind. He had known right from the start that it was far too easy hauling Gerry Brauner in. If he had been talking to a colleague, he would have called it lazy policing, grabbing the obvious option without thinking it through. As Colley had pointed out more than once, Brauner had earned plenty of money off Danny Galston's back down the years, why on earth would he kill him now when everyone knew the nationals kept coming back to the story time and time again? It made no sense. Maybe the lawyer was right, thought Blizzard sourly, maybe he was letting personal antipathy for the media influence his thinking.

As the chief inspector stared out of the window at the bare trees in the police station car park, his mind went back again to the murder of Jenny Galston and her young daughter. Perhaps he was looking in the wrong place, perhaps the death of Danny Galston was not about Brauner or Cargill, perhaps it was really about what happened that night 15 years ago. Perhaps this was the unfinished business that had preyed on the chief inspector's mind for so long.

The chief inspector's reverie was disturbed by the return of Colley, who walked into the office and slumped into a chair.

'What do you reckon?' asked Blizzard.

'Slippery customer, our Mr Brauner.'

'Yeah, but there's no way he killed Danny Galston.'

There were a few moments' silence then the sergeant looked at Blizzard uncertainly.

'I wonder if I can have a chat.'

'The weather or the rugby results?' said Blizzard, sensing that this was the moment Colley was going to unburden himself about Jay's pregnancy.

'Neither,' said Colley, managing only the weakest of smiles. 'Something a bit more important than rugby.'

'More important than rugby?' said Blizzard, feigning amazement then, on seeing the sergeant's uncomfortable expression, becoming serious again. 'Go on, David, spit it out.'

'Well,' said the sergeant, taking a deep breath. 'Three months ago…'

There was a knock on the door and in walked Arthur Ronald.

'Morning, gentlemen,' said the superintendent, settling himself down in a seat. 'How's it going?'

'Later, David,' said Blizzard, giving Colley a reassuring smile. 'We'll talk about it later. I promise.'

The sergeant nodded and left the room.

'Did I come in the middle of something?' asked the superintendent when he had gone.

'Just a discussion about the weather,' said Blizzard.

'I won't ask,' said Ronald, looking bewildered. 'How did it go with Brauner?'

'There's no way he killed Danny Galston.'

'Pity. The chief is never off the phone about it and the press are hassling us for something new. Anything in mind?'

'I reckon we should re-open the investigation into the Galston deaths.'

'Keep it uncontroversial, why don't you?' said Ronald bleakly. 'Why do you want to re-open it?'

'I think we both know the answer to that, Arthur.'

'I suppose,' said Ronald, 'but I'll need a better story than that.'

'Just tell the chief this is a chance to solve the crime without worrying about injunctions.'

'Not sure he will buy that.'

In the years since he had become CID chief for the area, the superintendent had broached the matter several times with the chief constable but each time had found himself rebuffed, and never with a straight answer.

'Besides,' continued Ronald, 'I may have something that could change your thinking. I have just come off the phone from the Regional Organised Crime Unit. Some DCI called Wendy Talbot. From West Yorks. Says she knows you.'

'Only a little,' said Blizzard, shifting in his chair and feeling a sudden shot of pain from his back.

'Still having problems?'

'You could say that,' said Blizzard. 'Anyway, yeah, I know Wendy Talbot. Decent cop. What did she want?'

'Seems Colley turned up at Galston's depot early this morning.'

'How come the Regional Organised Crime Unit know about that?' asked Blizzard.

'I'll tell you in a minute. What was he doing there?'

'I sent him round to have a chat with Ralph Cargill about the dust-up with Gerry Brauner but he was out on a run. We'll try again later.'

'Might I suggest you don't.'

'What the hell is that supposed to mean? And how come the Unit are sticking their nebs in?'

'Their surveillance team saw Colley arrive,' said Ronald.

'What sodding surveillance team?' exclaimed Blizzard.

'They've been watching the haulage depot for two months.'

'Nice of them to tell us! I thought we'd sorted this out after that balls-up on the Greentree estate last year.'

'It seems old habits die hard,' said Ronald.

'Clearly. Why are they interested in the haulage depot?'

'They reckon Galston and Cargill have been using their lorries to bring in guns.'

'Marvellous,' said Blizzard. 'So, Colley could have had his head blown off?'

'There's a link to some gang in Moscow, apparently. According to Wendy Talbot, they're pretty sure one of the guns was used to kill that security guard in Leeds this summer.'

'I remember it. Bank job.'

'Yes, it was. Guard fought back and they shot him. Anyway, Wendy is coming over to brief us this afternoon. How come you know her?'

'I met her when you forced me to go to that crappy seminar in Nottingham last year.'

'Such an enlightened attitude to career advancement,' said Ronald. 'Anyway, I want you to keep Colley away from Ralph Cargill until then. Softly-softly and all that. Oh, and behave yourself when Wendy turns up.'

'Would I let you down?'

Ronald decided not to answer.

'One more thing, Arthur,' said Blizzard as the superintendent headed for the door. 'The Galston case? Can I re-open it?'

'If you must,' said Ronald. He turned back and lowered his voice to a conspiratorial whisper. 'But these are dangerous waters, you know that more than most. Make it look like it's part of the inquiry into Danny's death, eh? Subtlety, John, subtlety.'

'I'll look it up in a dictionary,' promised Blizzard solemnly.

Chapter seven

Cara Galston had been enjoying a good morning. The stream of well-wishers who had been regularly turning up to irritate her with their platitudes – few of her friends liked Danny – had dried to a trickle, Georgia had undertaken to organise the funeral and her accountant had confirmed that her share of the haulage business would be worth well over £10m. It had struck Cara, as she spoke to him on the phone that morning, that the accountant was uneasy at being asked the question so soon after Danny's death but if he had concerns, he kept them to himself. Cara hoped he would also keep his mouth shut if the police came calling. Such a revelation would not look good at a time like this. Nevertheless, she thought, as she sat in the lounge, feet up on the pouffe and sipping a cup of mid-morning peppermint tea, everything was going very well, all things considered. Indeed, Cara had never realised grief could be this enjoyable.

She sighed as her reverie was interrupted by the door bell and she padded her way through to the hallway and opened the front door, expecting to see one of her so-called friends clutching a bunch of flowers and bearing a fixed expression of what they believed to be sympathy.

Instead, she was confronted by an unshaven man who looked like he had not been to bed.

'Where have you been?' said Cara irritably as Brauner walked in. 'I've rung loads of times but there's been no answer.'

'The police lifted me last night.'

'Do they know about us?' she said quickly.

'That's the least of our problems. Lenny's back.'

The blood drained from Cara Galston's face and she felt her legs shaking.

Chapter eight

'Look, I don't want this to turn into a slanging match,' said DCI Wendy Talbot as she sat in Arthur Ronald's office that afternoon.

'I am just saying,' remarked Blizzard, ignoring the superintendent's disapproving expression, 'that we are supposed to be on the same side yet now we hear that your lot have been skulking about for weeks without telling us.'

'I hardly think skulking is the right word,' said Talbot. 'This is a major surveillance operation.'

'So why not tell us about it then? I mean, it is our patch, for God's sake.'

'I appreciate that, John, but we could not risk word getting out.'

'Are you saying we cannot be trusted?' asked Blizzard sharply, 'because that is certainly...'

'Enough,' said Ronald, holding up a hand. 'We're getting nowhere slagging each other off.'

Blizzard muttered something that neither of the officers heard but Wendy Talbot did not reply; she knew better than to get into a fight with John Blizzard, particularly when she needed his support. Aged in her late-forties, she was a deceptively slight woman with short brown hair starting to grey at the temples and narrow, angular features which gave her a sharp appearance, an image she fostered among colleagues. Those who knew her well saw the softer, more human, side – mother of two teenagers, wife of a workaholic businessman recovering from a mild stroke and a keen golfer who despaired of ever finding the time to play – but within the Regional Organised Crime Unit it was a side she kept well hidden. Wendy Talbot had experienced too much resentment from successful senior women officers down the years to risk showing any signs of weakness.

There were some female officers who would put John Blizzard in the misogynist category, who would describe him as man unable to cope with high-flying women, but Wendy Talbot read him differently. Having spent a day with him on a training course and listened to his common-sense words amid the senior officers' jargon, it seemed to Talbot that she and John Blizzard were not that different, that all they did was tell it as they saw it.

Talbot also knew that on several occasions down the years, Blizzard had rebuffed approaches to join the Unit. The chief inspector's persistent refusals intrigued Wendy Talbot and now she resolved to be conciliatory.

'I am prepared to admit we got it wrong,' she said. 'We should have told you what was happening. It's just...'

She hesitated. Could she really afford to be totally honest with them? For all her admiration for Blizzard, she had only met him once and had only just been introduced to Arthur Ronald. Reputation said the superintendent was a decent and honest man but Wendy Talbot had learned to trust only her own officers. And then not even all of them. She studied the expectant detectives for a moment. Time to take the risk, she decided.

'We think they may have someone on the inside,' she said.

'With the police?' asked Blizzard.

'Possibly.'

'Now, come on, Wendy,' said Ronald, reacting the same way he always did whenever such suggestions were made, 'I cannot really believe that...'

'Hear her out, Arthur,' said Blizzard.

Talbot gave him an appreciative look. As she began to talk, Blizzard's thoughts went back to Harry Roberts' subtle intimation that someone powerful was protecting Danny Galston. He leaned forward in his chair to listen closer.

'We believe the guns are being brought into the UK by a Leeds gang,' said Talbot. 'We think they have linked up with a Russian who is buying weapons from demobbed soldiers. Moscow police have been watching him for a while.'

'It's a long way from Moscow to Hafton,' said Blizzard. 'Any proof?'

'We thought so. Two months ago, we raided a warehouse in Leeds where our informant said the gang were storing the weapons. It was supposed to be the end of the operation. Once we had gone in, the Russian police were going to make the arrests at their end. But, surprise, surprise, the place was empty.'

'Your information could have been wrong,' said Ronald.

'Our contact was definite about it. Besides, the place had been cleared out in a hurry. Twice since then, we have tried to mount ops only for the gang to change their plans at the last minute. I am sorry, but we have to consider the possibility that someone is feeding them information.'

'Any idea who?' asked the superintendent.

'No. Don't look like that, John. It's the God's honest truth.'

'That's why I never fancied the Regional Organised Crime Unit,' said Blizzard drily. 'Too much religion.'

Talbot laughed: the comment had eased the tension.

'So where exactly do Galston and Cargill fit into this?' asked Ronald. 'I would not have thought either of them were big league.'

'One of our surveillance teams followed your guys to a house in Leeds owned by one of the gang. Turns out he and Cargill have known each other since school. We are pretty sure the lorries are bringing the guns through Hafton docks. And both Cargill and Galston do regular trips to Moscow.'

'But now Danny Galston is dead,' said Blizzard.

'And we wonder if the Eastern Europeans found out he was an ex-copper and decided to get rid of him.'

'Danny Galston was the last person on earth to help the police,' said Blizzard.

'The gang might not have been as easily convinced.'

'So, when are you going in?' asked Ronald.

'Monday. We believe Cargill plans to move a batch of weapons then.'

'But in the meantime,' said the chief inspector, 'I still have a murder inquiry to run. It'll look a bit strange if we keep away. Danny Galston was Cargill's partner, after all.'

'I appreciate that but who knows?' There was a twinkle in Talbot's eye. 'If you give us a day or two, we might solve your case for you as well.'

The comment stayed with Blizzard for the rest of the day because it was exactly what he would have said.

Chapter nine

'We're re-opening our inquiry into the murders,' said Blizzard.

The words hung heavy in Cara Galston's living room. It was late that afternoon and sitting on the sofa were the widow, relaxed and dressed tastefully in dark slacks and a red blouse with several buttons undone, and an anxious Georgia Horwood. Blizzard and Colley had met her several times over the years as part of their inquiries into the attack on Jenny Galston and her daughters. However, sitting there now, it struck her that they hardly knew her at all. Georgia was about ten years older than Cara and as big a contrast as could be imagined, a prim self-contained woman with straight brown hair, cut short but without much in the way of styling, and wearing a brown skirt and a pale green cardigan over her starched white blouse. It seemed to the officers that Georgia had always presented an image of a woman who had grown old before her time. Some said she aged the moment Jenny and her godchildren were attacked. Certainly, as the detectives looked at her now, they sensed Danny's death had brought back painful memories.

'May I ask why you would want to re-open the case?' asked Georgia. 'It can only re-open old wounds, especially at a terrible time like this.'

'Whoever killed Danny did that for us, Miss Horwood,' said Blizzard.

Georgia digested the comment. Cara said nothing but stared out of the window, almost as if the conversation was of no relevance to her. The detectives realised that might actually be the case: she had never shown any interest in what had happened to Jenny and her children. Indeed, it had seemed to them that Cara Galston had done her best to airbrush Danny's family out of his history. Instinctively, Blizzard glanced at the mantlepiece and the wedding photograph of Cara and Danny. The detectives sensed that, on the other hand, not a day went by without Georgia recalling the lost ones. She seemed close to tears.

'Nevertheless,' she said, trying to regain her composure, 'I cannot see that re-opening the case will serve any useful purpose.'

'I can assure you that we have not taken this decision lightly,' said the chief inspector, 'but we would not be doing our jobs if we did not at least consider the possibility that Danny's death is linked in some way.'

'I fail to see how that could be,' said Georgia. 'Jenny and the poor children passed away many years ago.'

'Pauline has never been confirmed as dead,' said Blizzard.

'I think that we all know that she passed over to the other side a long time ago.'

Blizzard's mind went back to Hafton Cemetery and the strange little girl standing beneath the trees, surveying him with those lifeless eyes.

'But she is not at peace yet,' he murmured, without realising he had said it.

'And just what do you mean by that?' asked Georgia.

'I mean that we need to close the case once and for all.'

'I thought you already had done that,' said Cara, unable to conceal the contempt in her voice. 'You made no secret of the fact that you thought Danny had killed them. Harry Roberts certainly thought so and you are no different.'

'But Danny always denied it.'

'Fine time to decide he's innocent, Chief Inspector,' said Cara with a dry laugh.

'I didn't say he was, but if either of you know anything that might cast some light on things, now is the time to speak up. Danny has gone now. Perhaps that changes things?'

Cara shook her head and Georgia looked out of the window.

'Miss Horwood?' asked Colley, noticing the gesture.

'Nothing.'

'Look,' said Colley, 'we are as desperate as you to bring this to an end so if there is anything that you can say now to help us bring...'

'Georgia has already said she knows nothing,' said Cara, glaring at the sergeant. 'I think you had better respect that, particularly at this difficult time.'

'Yes, but...'

'And I am sure your superior officers would not take kindly to the harassing of a poor, grieving widow, Sergeant.'

Colley glanced at Blizzard, who shrugged.

* * *

A few minutes later, the detectives were back on the front drive. Blizzard unlocked the car door then turned and stared back at the house. Georgia was watching him out of the living room window but turned away when she saw him looking at her.

'What are you thinking?' asked Colley.

'Secrets, it's always bloody secrets with that lot.'

'They're certainly covering something up,' said the sergeant. He lowered himself into the passenger seat.

'Listen,' said the chief inspector, getting into the driver's seat and wincing as his back twinged, 'I want you to review all the evidence from the original murders. Tell me if we missed anything.'

He reached into his jacket pocket as his mobile telephone started ringing.

'Blizzard,' he said.

'It's Randall,' said the gravelly voice belonging to one of the detective sergeants over on the east side. 'We need to meet.'

Blizzard listened for a few more moments then replaced the phone in his pocket.

'Well, well, well,' said the chief inspector. 'The game's back on.'

Chapter ten

'Sorry, guv,' said Colley, looking up wearily from the documents he had been studying all morning as Blizzard walked into the deserted CID squad room. 'I can't see anything here.'

Blizzard dragged a chair over and sat down at the other side of the desk.

'Nothing at all?' he asked.

'You know Harry. He covered all the angles.'

'He always did play things by the book, but is there still not a chance that we missed something?'

'If we did, I can't see it,' said Colley, looking back down at the case file on the deaths of Jenny and Chloe Galston.

'And Ralph Cargill wasn't much help, as I recall.'

'Said he had no idea who would want to hurt them. Do you want me to mention it when I see him?'

'Mention nothing. Make it look routine.'

Colley nodded. The chief inspector, trusting Colley implicitly, had told him about the gun-running investigation the moment he left the meeting with Wendy Talbot the afternoon before, stressing the need for a sense of circumspection until the raid was carried out the following Monday. While understanding the reason for the cautious approach, Colley shared the frustration felt by his colleague. It was, as the sergeant had said over an after-work pint, like working with one arm tied behind their backs.

* * *

Colley arrived at the headquarters of GC Haulage on the small Hafton West Industrial Estate shortly after three-thirty that afternoon. Standing at the end of the estate furthest from the main road, and backing onto the canal, the garage and single-storey office block were home to a business that had been built up by Galston and Cargill until it had an annual turnover running into several millions.

The sergeant edged his car through the green gates and into a high-walled yard strewn with broken crates, tools and coils of wire. Colley parked in between two large lorries being loaded by a team of workmen and headed for the office block and up the stairs to the office. He was received courteously by Ralph Cargill, a man in his fifties with thinning grey hair, a neatly-cropped grey beard and a wiry frame which indicated someone who looked after himself. Even though he was dressed in oil-stained blue overalls, he had a more urbane demeanour than the boorish Danny Galston and as Colley took a seat amid the overflowing files and scruffy ledgers piled up on the floor of the office, the sergeant was struck by the contrast between the men.

'I wondered when you'd come,' said Cargill.

'I tried yesterday, Mr Cargill.'

'I've been very busy.'

'Even at a time like this?'

'I still have to keep the business running,' said Cargill. 'I took on a couple of Danny's runs. Been over to Mansfield. I assume you have come about his death?'

'I am trying to piece together a picture of his life.'

'Surely you have all the information you could ever need. Your lot have been hassling him for years.'

'Nevertheless, you might know something of use to us.'

'Danny was a very private man.'

'He did not strike me like that,' said the sergeant.

'It was all front. He was really ill at ease with people. I deal with the clients, Danny just liked driving lorries.'

'But…'

'You are wasting your time here, Sergeant. Danny Galston was not a man given to revealing much of himself, certainly not to me.'

'Surely, as his closest friend…'

'Who said we were friends?'

'You had been in business for more than twenty years.'

'My milkman has been delivering yoghurts to my house for thirty-five years but it does not mean we go on holiday together,' said Cargill, smiling at his joke. 'I'd go out to the odd official "do" with Danny, maybe have a couple of pints afterwards, but that was about it.'

Colley eyed the haulier, trying to work out if he was telling the truth. There was something self-contained about the man, a sense that his defences were well and truly employed but that behind the calm and measured answers, there was a lot going on. The sergeant could hear Blizzard's voice in his head. *'Secrets,'* it said. *'Always secrets'.* However, mindful of Blizzard's demand for circumspection, Colley decided to play the unimaginative copper and keep his thoughts to himself.

'Had Danny been worried about anything?' he asked.

'He was always upset when the anniversary came around. Not helped by Gerry Brauner. I assume you know about him?'

'I know you broke his camera.'

'He was lucky I didn't break his bloody neck. Greasy little shit. Wanted me to set up Danny. Tried it every year.'

'But you didn't?'

'Listen, Sergeant, it's no secret that myself and Danny did not get on but there was no way I was going to play Brauner's game.' He glanced at his watch. 'I have a couple of trucks to get off otherwise we'll miss the ferry. Have we finished?'

'Just one more thing – do you think Gerry Brauner could have killed Danny? His pictures show that he was there at the time.'

'Typical of the man,' said Cargill. He opened the window and yelled down to one of the workers in the yard. 'Roy, get a sodding move on, they won't put themselves in the truck!'

He slammed the window.

'No, Gerry would not kill him,' he said. 'Why kill the fatted calf? Now, you really must go. If we miss the ferry there will be hell to pay.'

* * *

At the same time as the sergeant was being ushered from the depot, the interview having come to its abrupt end, Blizzard was heading for Hafton Cemetery four miles away. As dusk descended on the city once more, the chief inspector pulled his car off the busy main road and edged up to the wrought-iron gates. Seeing them closed, he honked his horn several times. While he waited, he surveyed the house at the entrance. It was a small Victorian stone-built affair with the light in its front window giving it a cosy air amid the deepening chill of the November evening. After a few moments, a figure emerged from the front door and walked towards the car. Blizzard wound down the window and looked into the face of Desmond Roach.

'Oh, it's you,' said the cemetery manager brusquely.

'Still in a job then?'

'No thanks to you. I'm on a final warning. What do you want?'

'I want to see the grave again.'

'Well you can't. Can't you read?'

Roach pointed to the large sign next to the entrance. *Closed at dusk*, it said.

'I don't do closed,' said Blizzard. 'Open the gates.'

'But my boss said…'

'I don't do bosses either. Open the gates.'

Roach hesitated but something in the chief inspector's expression made him bite his tongue. Ten minutes later, Blizzard was standing in front of the Galston grave. Throughout his career, he had always told his officers to let the scene talk to them. It was all too easy to become so engrossed in an inquiry that they failed to see the bigger picture. Stand back and it was amazing what was revealed. That's what Harry Roberts had taught Blizzard, and he often passed it on to his officers. He had lost count of the times it had worked for him and it happened again now as he stood at the grave, letting his mind roam in its search for answers. The more it roamed, and the more he looked at the beaming face of little Chloe looking up at him out of the gravestone, the more Blizzard instinctively knew that Danny's death was nothing to do with gun-running.

'Unfinished business,' he murmured.

Oblivious to the cold starting to wheedle its way into his bones – the chief inspector was not wearing a coat – Blizzard's mind went back to those dark days 15 years previously. It was easy to see why the officers in the case had felt Danny Galston was guilty of slaughtering his family. The haulage boss had been apprehended five hours after the killing, and during several subsequent interviews his story never changed. In his version, Danny had been upstairs running a bath for Chloe, when he heard a commotion in the living room.

Hearing screams from his wife downstairs, Galston rushed out onto the landing but was confronted by a masked man brandishing a knife. The man demanded to know where the safe was and said everyone knew Danny had money. Galston claimed that he struck out at the intruder and that a struggle ensued. As the two men fought, Chloe and Pauline ran out onto the landing from their bedrooms and started to scream. Galston claimed that, as he half-turned, the intruder dealt him a savage blow to the head, which sent him tumbling down the stairs, smashing his right cheek on the wall as he fell. At the bottom, Galston was vaguely aware of Pauline running out into the street and crying for help. Galston said that, as he struggled to his feet, he became aware of a terrible silence in the living room and a second masked man ran out into the hallway and lashed out a foot, sending Danny Galston flying backwards once more. By now in great pain and not really knowing where he was, Galston stumbled out into the street and the next thing he knew was when two uniformed officers arrested him as he wandered on the edge of the city centre later that evening.

It was a story that never wavered through long hours of questioning and certainly Danny Galston's shock had seemed genuine enough. Standing now by the grave, Blizzard remembered him breaking down in the interview room and sobbing. The medical examiner did later confirm that Galston had been struck in the face. Pushed hard by Harry Roberts, the examiner had been unable to rule out that the injury was self-inflicted. Unlikely, the doctor had said, unhappy at the way he felt Roberts was trying to pressure him, but not impossible.

The chief inspector now found himself, and not for the first time in recent days, viewing the events differently. He remembered the fierce way Harry Roberts had conducted himself, never sleeping, drinking too much, pushing, pushing, always pushing for a breakthrough. But what if he had pushed too hard, wondered Blizzard? What if they had all pushed too hard? What if they had not taken that moment to stand back as he was doing now, but had instead let their feelings take over in their desperation to avenge the death of Chloe Galston? Blizzard gave a small shake of the head as if to banish the memories but the thoughts kept crowding back and among them were the words of Desmond Roach when he said that Danny Galston came every year to place flowers on the grave. What if the detectives had made a terrible mistake. What if? What if? What if? No, Danny Galston had killed them and that was all there was to it.

Blizzard frowned when he noticed that the red paint had not been cleaned off the Galston gravestone properly. Resolving to confront Roach about his shoddy work, he turned and gave a start; picking its way silently between the trees and the gravestones, was a figure. Blizzard gave a sharp intake of breath then relaxed when he recognised Gerry Brauner.

For his part, when Brauner spied Blizzard standing by the grave, he considered leaving but something made him keep walking. The truth was that Brauner had found himself moved by the death of Danny Galston in a way he had not expected. A man used to cynically dealing with tragedies as good stories to be sold at the highest price, he knew that sometimes they got through every journalist's defences. The killings of Jenny and Chloe Galston had certainly been one of those occasions and Danny's death had brought back unwelcome memories. At the time, Brauner had been a young staff photographer for the local evening newspaper and something about little Chloe's face beaming out of the front page had touched him, just as it touched everyone who saw it. Even though he had no children at the time, Gerry Brauner had cried for that little girl then and had done so more than once since, his emotions heightened down the years because he now had young children of his own. Brauner assumed that some cases also got to police officers; he had grown to know Harry Roberts a little down the years and recalled how the DCI struggled to talk about the case. Such feelings were, Brauner assumed, similar even for John Blizzard.

As Brauner approached the grave, he recalled the way such strong emotions had made his relationship with

Danny Galston a strange one. Although the haulage boss had threatened him with injunctions and to have him beaten up on more than one occasion, there had been a sort of acceptance that each man had a role to play in the drama. That it was part of the ritual. Or at least that was how Brauner had seen it, although he was honest enough to acknowledge that was probably a deluded attempt on his part to make himself feel less guilty.

Walking through the damp grass of the cemetery, Brauner again contemplated turning back. Maybe this was too risky, maybe Blizzard knew about his relationship with Cara. Maybe he knew what she had been up to. Then he noticed that the chief inspector had seen him, so Brauner took a deep breath and kept walking.

'You've got a nerve,' said Blizzard as the photographer approached the grave.

'No need for that.'

'So, what brings you here?'

Brauner did not reply.

'Your lawyer isn't here now,' said the chief inspector. 'You can talk freely if you want to.'

Blizzard surveyed the photographer for a moment: gone was Brauner's customary mocking smile, replaced by something more serious, sad even.

'Come on, Gerry. Time to stop holding out on me.'

'About what?'

'If I knew that...'

The men stood in uncomfortable silence for a moment, conscious of the thickening fog around them, wheedling its way in among the trees and shrouding the graves. Blizzard shivered.

'You got kids?' asked Brauner suddenly.

Blizzard shook his head. 'You?'

'Yeah, two. Eight and ten. Don't see as much of them as I should.'

'Too busy snatching pictures of innocent victims, I imagine,' said Blizzard, the edge back in his voice.

'You reckon Danny Galston was an innocent victim, do you?'

'Meaning?'

Brauner shook his head: he had already said too much.

'I could arrest you again,' said Blizzard.

'Wouldn't change anything.'

'So, what does bring you here? I can't see a camera bag.'

'Not sure. Just felt I had to come. You?'

'The same.'

'Maybe we're not that different after all, Blizzard.'

Another silence, this time slightly more comfortable. A sort of understanding.

'We need to go,' said Blizzard, glancing at his watch then nodding towards the cemetery entrance. 'Your little mate will be getting twitchy about his gates.'

Brauner nodded and started to walk away. Blizzard sensed someone behind him and swung round. There, over by the same gravestone as last time, stood the strange little girl in her white dress, her eyes lifeless as she surveyed him in silence. Heart thumping, the chief inspector took a step closer but she vanished into the mist.

Chapter eleven

Cara Galston drew the curtains to shut out the night. She was lying on the sofa in her softly-lit lounge, occasionally sitting up to reach out a hand to a side table and take a sip of a late afternoon Martini, while watching Countdown on the large-screen television she had had delivered the day before. It was a relief to have some time to herself because Georgia had spent much of the day with her, arriving just after eleven and only leaving about three. Cara had said little and Georgia had monopolised the conversation, explaining that the police believed Danny's body would be released inside a week for burial then going on to discuss the funeral service. Cara tried to look interested. Occasionally, Georgia would glance at the new television. Cara knew what the look meant and she explained that it had been ordered before Danny's death. It seemed to placate her friend, but not much. *What would the police think when they saw it?* she asked more than once.

After a while, Cara found the whole experience trying and, on the pretext of feeling weary and needing a lie down, she managed to persuade her friend to leave. Once Georgia had departed, Cara had poured herself the Martini, kicked off her slippers and settled down in front of the television. It was as she was wrestling with one of Carol Vorderman's mathematical puzzlers and debating whether or not it was too early to risk a second drink, that the phone rang. Cara sighed and padded out into the hallway.

'It's Gerry,' said the voice at the other end of the phone. 'I've just met Blizzard down at the cemetery.'

'And?'

'I reckon he knows more than he's letting on.'

'What did he say?'

'Nothing, just a feeling I got,' said Brauner.

'Just keep calm. Everything is going fine.'

She replaced the receiver and went back into the living room where she heard the scraping of shoes on gravel at the front of the house. Expecting another well-wisher, Cara sighed, placed the Martini out of sight behind the sofa, and walked over to the front window, peering through the curtains. Although the security light had come on, she could not see anyone at the door. Mystified, she looked across the garden and saw a shadowy shape over by the trees, concealed in the lee of the wall. Screwing up her eyes to see better, she realised that the person was heading down the side of the house. Cara ran frantically across the lounge and hurled herself into the kitchen, reaching desperately to lock the back door. But she was too late and the door slammed open, catching her a hefty blow to the head and sending her crashing backwards where she struck the fridge and slumped to the floor. Dazed, she opened her eyes and saw a bull-faced man standing over her.

'Oh, God,' she gasped, staring up into the features she had hoped never to see again.

'Surprise, surprise, Cara,' the man said, with a grin that showed crooked teeth.

'Get out, Lenny,' breathed Cara, surprising herself as she found new strength and started to struggle to her feet. 'I want nothing to do with...'

The blow from his meaty fist sent her slumping back against the fridge.

'One more sound and I'll kill you,' snarled Lenny Rowles.

She suddenly realised that he had produced a knife. The cry choked in her throat and she looked up at him fearfully and went quiet. You did not argue with Lenny Rowles.

'What do you want?' she croaked.

'I'm here to make sure you keep your mouth shut. I don't know what your game is but one word to the police and you're dead meat, Cara. Dead fucking meat. Tell Brauner the same.'

Rowles turned and slammed a gloved fist through one of the glass-fronted cabinets, shattering several of her prized ornaments. Cara screamed as he struck out again, sweeping several of her antique jugs off one of the shelves. Then he turned and snapped out a booted foot, catching her in the ribs and sending her reeling across the floor, shrieking with the pain like a wounded cur.

'So, just keep your mouth shut,' snarled Rowles. He crouched down so close that she could smell his fetid breath as he held the knife to her face so she could feel the chill of its blade.

'I will, Lenny.' Cara nodded, her eyes wide, her voice shaking. 'I will.'

Rowles gave a final leer, turned and disappeared into the night. Cara Galston lay amid the shattered wreckage of her kitchen for the best part of an hour, unable to move, waiting for her heart to stop pounding. Then the tears came, racking her body and stinging in her eyes. For Cara Galston, her husband's death had suddenly become a serious affair.

Chapter twelve

'Thanks for seeing me at such short notice,' said Blizzard, sitting in the doctor's surgery shortly after six that evening.

'It sounded urgent,' said the GP, a white-haired man in his early sixties. 'What's the problem?'

'It's happened again.'

'Same girl?'

Blizzard nodded.

'Interesting,' said the doctor.

'It's more than bloody interesting from where I'm sitting,' said Blizzard tetchily. 'I'm losing sleep over this.'

'As I recall,' said the doctor with a slight smile, 'you have not slept well for many years anyway. Perhaps you should consider alternative employment, John.'

Blizzard looked at him bleakly.

'According to this,' said the doctor, glancing down at the detective's case notes, 'you first came to me with this six weeks ago. So, when did you see her again?'

'Twice this week. One a couple of hours ago. Both times in the cemetery again.'

'The anniversary was this week, was it not?'

'I never miss it,' said Blizzard.

'Why not?'

Blizzard considered the question for a moment; it was not an easy one to answer. Or perhaps it was, if he was honest. Guilt took him there. Guilt that he had not brought the killer to book, guilt that he had not fulfilled his promise to Harry Roberts, guilt that Pauline Galston was out there somewhere and he had not found her. Guilt that he had cried for Chloe but not for her older sister. And now there was something else preying on the chief inspector's mind. A nagging feeling that perhaps he had read Danny Galston wrong for all these years. Blizzard hated the thought and found he could not find the words to answer the doctor's question.

'Well,' said the doctor, 'as I think I mentioned last time, the painkiller you are taking for your back can lead to hallucinations in rare circumstances.'

'But why her? How come I'm not seeing purple dinosaurs playing the banjo in the sodding high street?'

'Because purple dinosaurs can't play the banjo. At least not particularly well.'

Blizzard gave him a pained look.

'Sorry,' said the doctor. 'Look, I'm no psychiatrist – I can refer you to one if you wish…'

'No way! It's bad enough coming to see you.'

'I thank you for those kind words. They mean so much to a humble health professional such as myself. What I was going to say was that the mind works in strange ways and it seems to me that Pauline Galston has been increasingly occupying your thoughts, has she not?'

'Just a bit,' said the chief inspector.

'So, maybe the effect of the drug and your preoccupation with Pauline have combined to create these somewhat vivid hallucinations,' suggested the doctor.

'What can you do about it then?'

'I can change your prescription, but this painkiller is regarded as the best one for keeping a lid on your fibrositis and from the way you walked in here, I am guessing that your back continues to give you trouble.'

'Any other options?'

'Find Pauline Galston,' said the doctor.

* * *

Blizzard walked out of the surgery, deep in thought as he clutched his renewed prescription. Picking his way across the busy road, he saw Colley standing outside the chemist shop, eating a chocolate bar.

'How's the back?' said the sergeant.

'Shite.'

'Yet you never complain. It's a marvel, guv,' said the sergeant, walking over to the bin and dropping his chocolate wrapper into it. 'You're an example to us all.'

'Did you sort out that surveillance on Brauner?' asked Blizzard.

'Yeah,' said the sergeant, walking back. 'We're starting tonight. What exactly are we looking for?'

'Dunno.'

'Right, we'll look for one of those. What colour are they?'

Blizzard smiled this time and they walked into the chemists where the chief inspector handed over his prescription and was asked to wait while it was prepared. The detectives wandered over to the window and stared out at the headlights of the rush-hour traffic.

'I've been doing some more checking on those other vandalism attacks in the cemetery,' said Colley.

'And?'

'They're all linked. The first attack was six weeks ago, red paint again, the gravestone of a woman called Susan Graham. At first the name meant nothing but I did some more checking and it turns out she was Ralph Cargill's sister. And, get this, she was also the company secretary at CG Haulage. Died of breast cancer last year.'

'Now that is interesting,' said Blizzard.

'I'm only just warming up.' The sergeant lowered his voice as he noticed the women behind the counter watching them. 'The second attack was three weeks later, red paint again, one of their lorry drivers – chap called Ray Heskey. Died two years ago of a heart attack.'

'So, we may be looking at a vendetta against the company? That's good work, David. Mind, I hope you have not been queering things for the Regional Organised Crime Unit with all your questions.'

'I have been the soul of discretion, guv.'

'Pity,' said Blizzard, walking towards the counter as the chemist held up his medicine. 'I'd quite like to foul up one of their ops.'

Chapter thirteen

'Time to talk, Georgia,' said Blizzard.

'I imagine it is,' she said.

It was shortly after eight that evening and the chief inspector was sitting in the trim living room of Georgia Horwood's terraced house, cradling a cup of tea and studying her with interest. The strong sense that she was holding something back when they met at Cara's the day before had played on Blizzard's mind ever since and now he sensed once more that there were things she could tell him. But she had not taken him into her confidence for fifteen years so he had called at her house more in hope than expectation.

'Why are you really re-opening the inquiry into the murders?' she asked at last.

'Surely that is obvious.'

'You always thought that Danny killed them. Now he's dead, surely there is nothing left to investigate.'

'But what if he is dead because someone wanted revenge for the little ones.'

'Then they would have done it by now. No one could sit on that anger for fifteen years, Chief Inspector.'

'You have.'

'What do you mean by that?'

'Nothing.' Blizzard softened his tone. 'Nothing, Georgia. I am just saying that people react in different ways to grief. What is clear is that you have thought about this quite a bit.'

'Those children are never out of my mind,' she said quietly. 'Never.'

'Of course, all this is assuming that Danny was guilty,' said Blizzard.

'Has something happened to change your mind?'

'What do you think? Did Danny kill them?'

Georgia said nothing and Blizzard looked at her, seeking some clue from her features, hoping that her momentary loss of emotional control would encourage her to be more forthcoming. But the chief inspector found nothing; the barriers were back up. Secrets, thought Blizzard, always secrets.

'So,' repeated Blizzard. 'Do you think Danny killed them?'

'That you should say such a thing is somewhat ironic, do you not think? Your Mr Roberts would be turning in his grave, I think.'

'Everything needs to be considered,' said Blizzard. 'Can I take you back to that night, Georgia?'

'I wish you wouldn't.'

'I have to. I am re-examining everything about the case. You knew Jenny well. Did she ever say she was frightened by anything?'

'Only of Danny. He was a bully. Jenny said he hit her and the kids. With a belt.'

'Did she fear for her life?'

'No. She said Danny was always very sorry afterwards, promising not to do it again; that sort of thing. It was the same with Cara.'

'He hit her as well?'

'Yes.'

'Tell me about Cara. I have always wondered how come you are such good friends. She hardly seems your type.'

'She's not.' Georgia chuckled – it seemed out of character. 'You know we met in the dramatic society? Well, everyone used to say we were chalk and cheese. Cara would play the leading roles, sticking her boobs out everywhere and flirting with the men in the audience, and I'd be the scullery maid or something, scuttling in with my bucket and a fag in my mouth.'

'But you clearly get on?'

'Yes, we do.'

'Tell me about her and Danny. Did she love him?'

'I'd rather not say.'

'Why?'

Georgia sighed. 'Because she hated him.'

'Because he hit her?'

'Because he was an appalling man.' The words were spat out. 'She deserved so much better.'

'Did she hate him enough to kill him?'

Georgia shook her head vigorously. 'Not her style,' she said.

'Why did you not tell us he was beating Jenny and the kids when they were murdered?'

'I did not think it was relevant then and I do not think it is relevant now. Danny Galston did not kill Jenny and the kids.'

'But someone did.'

'They were such lovely children,' she said, her eyes moist with tears as emotion broke through. 'Chloe was a little sweetie.'

'And Pauline?'

'A strange little girl but once you got to know her, she was fine. Loved reading. Never happier than when she was locked away in her bedroom with her books.' She looked at the chief inspector intently. 'Do you think she is dead, Mr Blizzard?'

'I don't know.'

'You said she is not at peace. Why would you say a thing like that?'

'I should not have said it. Sorry.'

'But maybe you are right.'

There was a silence for a few moments.

'Georgia,' said Blizzard. 'I think Cara is holding out on me, I think Gerry Brauner is doing the same, and I think you are. Why won't people talk about this?'

She said nothing.

Blizzard sighed, drained his cup and left the house.

Chapter fourteen

There was an underlying tension that evening at Arthur Ronald's large detached home in an exclusive gated housing complex in one of the villages on the city's western edge. Sitting in his favourite armchair in his spacious cream-carpeted lounge, surrounded by French Impressionist prints and exotic ornaments gleaned from holidays around the world, the detective superintendent eyed the four men intently. The men behind Operation Keeper. Not that anyone else knew about its existence. Officially, the meeting was not even taking place and were Operation Keeper's existence to be uncovered before it could achieve its aims, all their careers would undoubtedly come to an abrupt end. Such a realisation had, as always, charged the atmosphere in the room. It had also bred a deep and abiding trust.

Sipping a glass of wine and studying each man in turn, Ronald knew their desire to crack one of the most baffling mysteries in the city's modern history was as strong as ever. Many cities have rumours of paedophiles at work in their shadows and Hafton was no exception. From time to time down the years, there had come tantalising reports of a group of influential men who paid for the provision of children for sex, both girls and boys. There was also rumours of children that had simply vanished. But each report was nebulous, fading like the mist, something intangible.

On taking command of Southern CID, Ronald had determined to solve the mystery and had broached his concerns with the chief constable. He found the chief reluctant to sanction an official inquiry, arguing that he was not prepared to release manpower or approve overtime budgets to deal with what he described as an urban myth. Faced with such unwillingness, Arthur Ronald took a decision that would have stunned those who regarded him as a cautious, even staid, individual; he launched a highly secretive investigation without official clearance.

Blizzard was one of the team in Ronald's living room, the chief inspector slumped in an armchair with his feet up on a stool to relieve the pain from his back. Over on the sofa was Colley, sipping at a can of lager. The sergeant looked weary, thought Ronald, his eyes tired and strained. The superintendent had noticed the fatigue several times in recent weeks but Colley had been evasive whenever questioned about it and Blizzard had feigned ignorance.

Beside the sergeant sat an officer in his early fifties, hair almost grey, thinning and cut short, his face chiselled and pock-marked, the eyes deep and dark. He was dressed in an ill-fitting navy black suit with no tie. He looked like the kind of man who did not even own a tie. This was Detective Sergeant Max Randall, a veteran who had worked with Ronald and Blizzard over at the Eastern Division in years gone by. On another armchair sat Alex Mather, a vice-squad detective in his late twenties who spent much of his time working undercover investigating crimes relating to the city's prostitution rackets. Slim with light brown hair, he was dressed in scuffed jeans and black T-shirt. Normally unshaven, he had grown a beard; none of the officers asked why as he sat quietly sipping his wine.

Despite the import of the gathering – it was the first time in seven months that they had all been together – the men had not discussed the sex ring in the hour they had been at the house. Their long-standing rule was that business must wait until they had eaten, and that Arthur Ronald had to pay for the food, so on the glass coffee table in front of them were several pizza boxes. Each officer had tucked into the meal with gusto: eating was one of the things that tended to be missed out on in the life of a Hafton detective.

'Lovely that was,' said Randall, finishing the last piece and reaching for his beer can.

'You are kidding, I take it?' protested Blizzard.

'I keep forgetting he's Egon-bloody-Ronay,' groaned Randall, winking at the grinning Colley. 'What's the problem, Jonny boy, the tomatoes not grown on the right Tuscan mountain slope for you?'

'I am just saying that if you knew anything about Italian cookery rather than being such a Philistine, you would…'

'Yeah, yeah,' said Randall, smiling as he placed his can back on the table.

'So why the call, Max?' asked Ronald, quickly placing a coaster beneath the sergeant's glass, bringing forth a smile from Randall.

'I've got a new informant. Met him in a boozer.'

'Truly a meeting of minds,' said Blizzard slyly. 'What did he want?'

'I thought he wanted to talk about a doorstep conman scam over on the Hawkmead Estate; he's been slipping me some useful stuff. Then he says something big is cracking off. Says the pub is not the place to talk. When I went to see him the next day, he was shitting himself. Wanted to know if he was promised immunity from prosecution if he gave me information about the sex ring.'

'And what did you say?' asked Ronald, topping up his glass of wine and offering the bottle around.

'Said I'd have to check it. You are the only I can turn to, Arthur.'

'And how exactly do you expect me to sanction something for an investigation that does not exist, Max? I mean, is this guy really worth sticking my neck out for?'

'I reckon he might be. I tell you, Arthur, I have never seen a man so scared. Something has spooked him and he's not alone.'

'I'll hazard a guess,' said Mather in his quiet Scottish lilt.

The others looked at him expectantly: Mather did not say much, so when he did, it commanded respect.

'The death of Danny Galston,' Mather said. 'Has to be. I'm hearing things as well. There's a few of my informants acting funny, looking over their shoulder all the time. It's like Danny's murder changed something. Who have you got in the frame for killing him, John?'

'The widow is the best bet. She's playing all sorts of games.'

'What if it's tied up with Keeper instead?' asked Mather. 'Don't tell me we haven't all considered the possibility that Danny is wrapped up in this.'

'Yeah, but we've gone back over all the old witness statements from 15 years ago,' said Colley. 'There's absolutely nothing to suggest that.'

'So we look deeper.'

It was unusual for Mather to be so assertive and they all looked at him. They knew why he was so keen to break open the ring and bring its leaders to justice. Like Randall – whose wife had taken their two teenage sons away several years before, complaining that he preferred the pub to his family's company – Mather had endured sadness in his home life. Several years before, unable to cope any more with his erratic lifestyle and the secrets it held, Mather's wife had returned to her mother, taking their baby daughter. The final straw had been when his daughter cried in terror when he walked in one night, with a straggly beard, after having gone missing unannounced for two weeks. All the officers knew that Mather had not seen his child since then, which was a driving factor in his involvement in Keeper. For Mather, it had always been about the children. For Mather, it was somehow about his child.

'OK,' said Ronald, placing his glass down on the coffee table. 'Let's assume Alex is right. Let's assume the murder of Danny Galston is tied up with Keeper, what exactly does that mean?'

'Maybe,' said Randall softly, 'it means it's endgame.'

Later that night, as he was clearing away the pizza boxes and empty glasses after everyone had gone home, it seemed to Arthur Ronald that Randall's words still hung heavy in the air.

Chapter fifteen

Next morning, Blizzard and Colley returned to the links between the attacks on the gravestones in Hafton Cemetery. Ten o'clock found them on one of the city's new housing estates, sitting in the living room of the detached house once shared by Brian Graham and his wife, Susan, former CG Haulage company secretary and Ralph Cargill's sister. The detectives were on a classy cool blue sofa, Graham on a matching armchair in a room that smacked of wealth.

The accountant was a grey-haired man in his mid-fifties, with a slightly owlish expression as he peered at them over round-rimmed spectacles, battling emotions stirred up by talking about his late wife. His smart attire could not conceal the tell-tale signs of a man facing difficulties. Glancing down at the fleck-covered carpet and over to the dusty sideboard, the detectives came to the conclusion that Graham was struggling to cope in the absence of his wife. A glance at the tin foil take-away meal cartons stacked up in the wastepaper bin confirmed their suspicions.

'My wife was a good woman,' said Graham, 'and what was done to her gravestone was an abomination.'

'Which is why we want to find out who did it,' said Blizzard.

'Have you ever seen anyone die of cancer, Chief Inspector?'

'I have,' nodded Blizzard, recalling that last night in the hospice with Harry Roberts. 'I would not wish it on my worst enemy.'

'So, you can see why I want you to catch the scumbag that vandalised Susan's gravestone.'

'Was it you who found the paint?'

'Yes. What kind of a person does a thing like that? I take it you think it has something to do with Danny Galston's murder?'

'Why do you ask that?' said Blizzard.

'It's been in the papers that you are leading the investigation. I can't see you being interested in vandalism otherwise. Perhaps whoever vandalised Susan's gravestone killed Danny.'

'Certainly, all three attacks had links to the company,' said Blizzard, glancing at Colley, who remained impassive apart from the merest raising of an eyebrow at the way Graham had been thinking things through.

'Three?' asked the accountant.

'Someone also threw paint over the Galston headstone and one belonging to one of the lorry drivers,' said Colley. 'Chap called Ray Heskey. Did you know him?'

'I didn't mix with any of the employees really. I did the company's accounts, that's about all.'

'You must have known Danny Galston pretty well?'

'Not really. We used to join them for the odd dinner, haulage association, that kind of thing. Sometimes we'd go for a late-night drink afterwards but it was not quite my scene. The pubs Danny liked were somewhat down-market.'

'I can imagine,' said Blizzard.

'Look,' said Graham, leaning forward in his chair. 'I do not want to talk ill of the dead but I assume you met Danny Galston?'

The detectives nodded.

'Then you know what he was like,' said Graham, warming to his theme. 'He was an arrogant man who thought money could buy him respect – forever flashing his cash. I warned him more than once that it was asking for trouble.'

'Was that the only reason you disliked him?' asked Colley.

'God, no. Look around you, Sergeant, I'm not short myself. When Susan became ill, Ralph was terrific, giving her time off, bringing in a temp to do some of her work, but Danny never made the slightest allowance, like he was making some kind of point. And he never even came to the funeral. Said he had a run to make. I would be lying if I said I mourned his passing.'

'What did you make of Cara?' asked the chief inspector.

'Now her I did like. Too good for Galston, mind, although more than one person has described her to me as a trophy wife. Seems a somewhat cruel description, although she is a very attractive woman.'

'She certainly is,' murmured Colley. The sergeant felt a stab of guilt as he thought of Jay lying in bed at home, pale as death after another bad night.

'Did you know Danny's first wife?' asked Blizzard, giving his sergeant a strange look.

'Jenny? Yes, met her a couple of times. A quiet woman.'

'And the kids?'

'Chloe was a little sweety. Always laughing.'

'And Pauline?'

'A strange little girl. Virtually never spoke.'

There was silence in the room for a few moments, broken only by the ticking of the clock on the mantlepiece.

'Can I say something?' asked Graham.

'Sure,' replied Blizzard.

'I know people say Danny killed them but even though I detested the man, I can't see that. He loved those kids, he really did.'

Blizzard tried to weigh up the contrast between the boorish haulier and the picture of a loving family man that was emerging. As ever, he found it impossible. Normally a man of certainties, the chief inspector found himself confused. Tough questions to be asked, he decided. Tough questions indeed.

Chapter sixteen

'So, what's she like?' asked Fee Ellis.

'Who?' said Blizzard.

'You know who. Wendy Talbot.'

It was later that evening and she and Blizzard were sitting in the corner nook of the chief inspector's local village pub. Blizzard was staring into the flames of the roaring fire and cradling a pint of beer in his hand while Fee sipped from a glass of white wine. Dressed in a dark jumper and jeans, she was five foot eight with a slight figure. Aged twenty-eight, she had a face that sometimes suggested someone cool, collected and unapproachable, at other times a person who was warm and animated. Also, on rare unguarded occasions, it suggested the vulnerability felt by a woman trying to survive in the man's world that was Hafton CID. That was why she was so interested to learn that Blizzard was working with Wendy Talbot. Fee knew she was regarded by many female officers as one of the pioneers in the tough world of CID in the northern forces and was intrigued.

'She's alright, I suppose,' said Blizzard, not sure what he was supposed to say.

'Oh, come on, you can do better than that, John.'

'Why so interested?'

'I'd quite like to know a bit about the woman my boyfriend plans to spend his night with.'

Blizzard chuckled. It had been agreed that he join Talbot and her team during the surveillance on the haulage depot the following evening, ahead of the Monday morning raid. It had been Talbot's idea, although she had acted partly out of purely selfish reasons, hoping the experience might give the chief inspector a taste for Regional Organised Crime Unit life. Blizzard had his own motives for agreeing to take part in the surveillance: he felt that involvement in the operation would allow him to make sure that the haulier was not spirited away beyond the reach of his questions.

'So, what *is* she like?' insisted Fee, a twinkle in her eye – she knew Blizzard was hopeless when it came to describing women. 'You are being distinctly evasive, my lad.'

'She's... you know.' Blizzard shrugged helplessly. 'OK.'

'OK what?' said Fee, taking another sip of wine. 'OK, a good copper. OK, a decent human being? OK, a right stotter and you wouldn't crawl over her to get to me?'

'I'm not sure that's the way to talk.'

'It's a simple enough question,' she said, trying not to laugh.

'Does it really matter?'

'I'm genuinely interested.' Fee suddenly looked serious. 'Any woman who gets to that high a rank has got to have something. I want to see what makes her special.'

'You're much prettier than her,' said Blizzard.

'Flattery will get you absolutely nowhere, Mr Blizzard,' she said, leaning over and kissing him gently on the cheek. 'Even bad flattery. So, come on, what *do* you make of her?'

The chief inspector took a gulp of beer and considered the comment; if there was one thing Wendy Talbot and Fee Ellis definitely had in common, it was the ability for straight-talking. Although he found it disconcerting at times, he had nevertheless always found it an attractive feature of women – his former wife had tended to talk more behind his back instead – so he pondered Fee's question for a few moments and resolved to tackle it head-on.

'I would have said,' he announced eventually, 'that she's more political than me but that in many ways we are similar.'

'So she's a good detective then?'

'Yeah, I reckon she is a good detective. However…'

'However, what?'

'However, she's wrong about Danny Galston. His death isn't about gun-running, I am sure of it.'

'But surely it makes perfect sense? I mean, he *was* a copper.'

'A long time ago. Besides, everyone knew Danny was ex-plod. I think it is more feasible that the gang liked the fact. Nothing better than a bent copper who knows all the tricks. No, there is something more personal to Danny's death than guns.'

'Like what?'

'I can't say.'

'Won't say, you mean.'

'No,' said Blizzard firmly, thinking back to the gathering in Ronald's house the night before. 'Can't. At least not yet.'

He wondered if he should tell her about Keeper. Wondered whether or not to confide in her about the strange little girl in the cemetery. Wondered if he should tell her that he doubted Danny Galston's guilt. In the end, the chief inspector decided not to. Somehow, it did not seem the time or the place.

'Let's talk about something else,' he said. 'Drink up. It's my round.'

* * *

The next morning dawned sharp and bright. Blizzard had worked a lot of overtime in recent weeks so Ronald had suggested that his reluctant DCI take the day off and leave the murder inquiry to his team. After a lazy couple of hours spent reading the Sunday papers in bed, Blizzard and Fee went for a bike ride. Blizzard had taken a fitness pledge more than a year before after being horrified by pictures of himself in the newspaper, clearly showing a double chin. His attempts to blame his embarrassment on a poor camera angle having brought forth only scepticism from colleagues, Blizzard had taken up swimming which helped but not enough. He knew he needed another way of taking off the pounds.

When he had started his relationship with Fee, he was initially perturbed to discover her love of cycling and in the first few months of their relationship had resisted whenever she tried to interest him in joining her on her rides. But after a lot of gentle badgering, and a bleak realisation that his middle-aged spread was spreading, he finally purchased a bike and, despite himself, found that he enjoyed cycling in the flat countryside around Haltby village, discovering new things about the area in which he lived each time they went out.

There were health benefits as well. This morning, he found to his relief that his back felt stronger than it had for several weeks and that the discomfort he had experienced on other rides had significantly receded. The freedom from pain and the effect of the bright sunshine did much to lighten the chief inspector's mood and he suggested lunch at the village pub before his visit to his elderly mother in a residential home in Hafton that afternoon. It was as the couple pulled up outside the pub that they saw David Colley, leaning against his car and grinning at the spectacle of the chief inspector on a bike.

'Bloody hell,' he said. 'If it isn't Eddy Merckx.'

'You can wipe that stupid grin off your face,' said the chief inspector.

'Sorry, guv.'

'No, you're not.'

Looking up from securing her chain and padlock round the bike's wheel, Fee laughed and the sergeant grinned again; he had always liked her and was delighted at the changes she had wrought in Blizzard. Before she arrived on the scene, the chief inspector had tended to be more introspective, more sour, but life with Fee had introduced him to laughter and a somewhat more relaxed approach to life.

'I take it the rugby went well then?' said the chief inspector, gesturing to the ugly bruise on the sergeant's cheek.

'Yeah. Walloped them. And I scored a try.'

'And that's good, is it?'

'Sure is.'

'So, what brings you out here?' asked Blizzard, cursing as he struggled with his bicycle chain then glancing over to the pub. 'Fancy a pint?'

'Er, no,' said Colley. 'Jay's not… well, you know…'

'The bug again?' said Blizzard noticing Fee's smile.

'Yeah, something like that. Look, can we talk?'

'Spit it out,' said Blizzard.

Colley hesitated and the chief inspector noticed his friend's unhappy expression.

'Come on,' said Blizzard. 'You can say it in front of Fee, you know that.'

'Don't worry,' said Ellis, sensing the sergeant's discomfort and heading into the pub. 'I'll see you in a few minutes, love.'

'What the hell was that about?' snapped Blizzard when she had gone. 'You know I have no secrets from…'

'Ah, but you have. Does she know about Keeper?'

Blizzard shook his head, calming down immediately.

'No,' he said. He patted his friend on the shoulder. 'I thought best not to tell her. Sorry for having a go. Come on, let's walk.'

When the officers had walked for a couple of minutes and had started to skirt the duck-pond on the village green, the sergeant began to speak, glancing round to make sure no one could overhear.

'I got a call last night,' he said in a low voice.

'From whom?'

'An informant. Bloke called Barry Lawson. He mentioned the murders fifteen years ago. Said he knows who the killer is.'

'Does he now?' said Blizzard with a low whistle. 'It certainly seems that the murder of Danny Galston has loosened some tongues.'

'My guy wants to see me tonight. Said he could not speak on the phone. Sounded really frightened. I thought you should know before I went.'

'Wise thinking. Who is this Lawson bloke then?'

'Used to work in social services before the smack got to him. Got himself sacked three years ago but I still reckon he knows plenty of things. So how do we play it?'

'I think that, first of all, you go home and spend some time with Jay since you are going to be out again tonight.'

'Yeah, she's made a couple of comments the last day or so.'

'I'm sure she has. Look, do you want me to talk to her, David, smooth things over?'

'No, she knows how it is. Thanks for the offer, though.'

'Do you want me to come with you tonight then? Ride shotgun?'

'There's no need for that. Barry's harmless enough. Besides, you need to get ready for the stake-out with your mate Wendy. Don't look so worried. I'll be alright.'

'Well, if you're sure.'

'Yeah, I'm sure,' said Colley and headed off towards his car. 'Enjoy your pint. And remember, you can be done for drunk-driving on a bicycle, you know.'

Blizzard chuckled and strolled back to the pub. When he and Fee emerged an hour later, someone had stolen his bike.

Chapter seventeen

Nine-thirty that night found David Colley standing on the edge of a playing field not far from one of the city's housing estates. It was where he normally met his informant and as he waited, leaning against the faded green sports pavilion with its window grilles and ugly graffiti, the sergeant could hear the faint sound of sirens in the city centre ten minutes' walk away. Looking out over the field, peering through the half-light offered by the street lights over on the main road, Colley could just make out the dim shapes of swings and the slide on the nearby children's playground, the equipment long since vandalised by groups of teenagers, the ground littered with beer cans, cigarette stubs and broken bottles.

The sergeant sighed at the sight. The thought of children took his mind back to the issue that had so occupied him over recent weeks. Stamping his feet to keep warm, he nostalgically recalled warmer climes. Although Colley's train of thought had started when he and Jay decided to try for a baby, his ideas had really crystallised during a holiday to Corfu a few weeks later – probably the time the child was conceived, the couple reckoned. Standing now, hearing in the near-distance the hum of mid-evening traffic punctuated by the occasional car horn, the sergeant found himself transported back to the couple's last night on the island.

Aware of the effect that holidays could have on the unwary, he had nevertheless spent the week increasingly thinking that he could so easily leave behind the murder and mayhem of his life in Hafton and live on the island, maybe running a bar, something like that. The thought had not been that well-formed until he discovered that the owner of their favourite bar was a former Met detective who had thrown it all in at the age of thirty-nine – just a little bit older than Colley. Colley had mentioned the idea of emigration to Jay on that last night in the bar. He did so tentatively; Jay, a willowy redhead in her early thirties, was Hafton born-and-bred, loved her job teaching at one of the city's primary schools and had resisted several job opportunities elsewhere in the past.

What had prompted his idea, Colley told her that night, emboldened by several glasses of red wine, was that he found himself increasingly obsessed with thoughts about the dark world into which they would bring their child. He knew a police officer's view was always more jaundiced than most people – the reason he had resisted the idea of a baby for so long – but listening to the lapping waves, the thought of bringing his child up abroad just would not go away. Jay had let him talk, ordered another bottle of wine and they had discussed the possibility for the best part of two hours, the conversation going round in endless circles without coming to any firm resolution as the sun set over the Mediterranean.

Standing on the playing field, the sergeant was so engrossed in his thoughts that he did not hear Barry Lawson approaching until alerted by the scrape of his informant's footfall on the nearby path.

'Bloody hell, man,' murmured Colley to himself. 'Keep your mind on the job.'

'That you, Dave?' came a voice.

'Yeah.'

Out of the shadows stepped a scruffy man, his face thin and sallow, the black hair lank and greasy, the clothes dirty and tatty, his anorak dirty and ripped on one shoulder.

'You look like shite, Barry,' said Colley.

'Thanks,' grunted the man as they started walking along the path which skirted the housing estate.

'Did you go to that drugs rehab centre?'

'Not yet.'

'For God's sake, Barry, if you don't get some help, you'll kill yourself.'

'Unless someone one else does first,' said Lawson.

'Is that what you wanted to talk to me about?'

'Maybe – what's it worth?' He sounded desperate. 'I need some cash.'

'I'll smooth that over once I know how good the information is. But not if you stick it in your arm, Barry. I've told you that before. If you do that, all bets are off.'

The informant hesitated.

'I'm serious, Barry,' said the sergeant. 'I want you to get help.'

'Yeah, OK, Dave.'

They both knew Lawson did not mean it but Colley elected not to pursue the matter: there were bigger things at stake than the well-being of a junkie.

'So, what have you got for me?' asked the sergeant as they walked across grass already starting to crunch with the evening frost.

'I take it you've heard the rumours about a sex ring in the city?'

'Yeah, but all I've heard are rumours. For all I know, it's all a load of cobblers.'

'It isn't.'

'What do you know?'

'You hear things.' The reply was suddenly evasive as if Lawson had realised the import of what he was doing.

'What things, Barry?'

'Things.'

'Look,' said Colley. 'I'm freezing my nuts off out here, you'd better give me something good or I'm off. How come you know things?'

'I've made some mistakes, that's all I'm saying.'

'Were you part of the ring?'

'Will you do me if I was?'

'Depends what you say, Barry. Were you part of the ring?'

'I was kinda on the edge of it.'

'For God's sake,' said Colley.

'I didn't do no abusing, honest. You know I was a social worker once? Well, I used to, you know, recruit some kids. From care homes, you know. But I never touched them, and that's the God's honest truth.'

'It still makes you as bad as the rest of them,' said Colley.

'You're right,' said Lawson. He stopped walking and stared at the sergeant. 'I'm not proud of what I've done and I'll tell you everything.'

'Why do that after all this time?'

'Same reason I found the kids. I need the money. I'm desperate, Dave. Fucking desperate. I owe some people, you know. I want police protection. One of them witness protection schemes.'

'I'm not sure…'

'This ain't some bunch of toe rags flogging knocked-off car stereos,' said Lawson. 'They would kill me if they knew I was talking to you.'

'Who would?' asked Colley, voice betraying his eagerness. 'I need names.'

Lawson hesitated again.

'OK,' said Colley. 'Let me start with one who can't hurt you. Danny Galston.'

'Yeah, him. But there's something you need to know as well. See, something has happened that has changed everything.'

'Like what?'

Before Lawson could reply, his eyes grew wide as he noticed a movement behind the sergeant.

'Jesus!' screamed Lawson and started to run.

Colley whirled round in time to see a bulky man looming out of the shadows wielding what looked like a knife. Colley yelled out and threw up an arm to protect himself as the man brought the knife down. Reacting instinctively, the sergeant threw himself to one side and lashed out a fist, bringing a pained grunt from the man as he staggered backwards, hand clapped to the side of his face. Colley seized the advantage and hurled himself at the man, striking out again and sending the knife flying. Caught off-balance, the assailant slipped on the icy grass and sunk briefly to one knee. Colley jumped forwards but yelled in pain as the assailant launched himself upward and head-butted the sergeant in the face. The sergeant staggered backwards, disorientated and desperately trying to clear the blood now pouring into his eyes from a gash to the forehead. When his sight cleared, the assailant had gone and so had Barry Lawson.

'I'm getting too old for this,' muttered Colley, reaching into his trouser pocket for his handkerchief and dabbing the wound.

Wearily, and with his head throbbing and stomach churning, the sergeant walked slowly towards the main road.

Chapter eighteen

It took a lot to worry Gerry Brauner, but he could feel the walls of his life crowding in as he arrived at Cara Galston's house shortly after eight the following morning to be confronted by the widow in her dressing gown, sporting an ugly bruise on her right cheek, her eyes bloodshot through lack of sleep and one arm heavily bandaged. Ushering him reluctantly into her living room, she sat down on the sofa and he noticed how her usual confidence had drained away. It seemed as if suddenly Cara Galston realised she was playing a dangerous game and it had frightened her. Looking at her battered features, it frightened Gerry Brauner as well.

'Who did this?' he asked, sitting down on an armchair.

'I think we both know that.'

'Are you sure it was Rowles?'

She nodded.

'I take it you have not been to the police?' said Brauner.

'Give me some fucking credit, Gerry!'

'So, what have you told people?' he asked, gesturing to the injuries.

'Said I fell off a chair reaching for a top cupboard.'

'Anyone believe it?'

'They never believed it when Danny thumped me, why should they do so now?' she said. 'I told Georgia what really happened, of course.'

'Are you sure that was wise, Cara?'

'She's not let us down so far, has she?'

Brauner gave a heavy sigh. His unease had been growing throughout the weekend, during which he had received several threatening calls, each one increasing in intensity as the man sought his continued silence in the face of intense police activity in the city. The man had heard the stories of detectives visiting informants, turning the pressure on in their search for a breakthrough, and had become increasingly worried as the days passed. But it was more than worry, thought Brauner. Behind the man's voice he thought he could detect fear. The police had never got this close. That was why Lenny Rowles had been brought back to the city.

'So, what are you going to do?' asked Brauner.

'Get out as planned. Just do it earlier. I've already told the estate agent to put the house on the market.'

'Make sure they don't put up any signs.'

'I'm not stupid!' snapped Cara. 'Sorry, this has got me pretty scared. Nobody expected Lenny Rowles to come back.'

Brauner nodded; he and Cara had discussed the idea of escaping abroad many times. For Brauner, who had reported on many of the biggest crime stories of the city's recent history, the days since Danny Galston's death had made him realise it was time to go. The news that Lenny Rowles was back had sent a shiver of fear through the city's underbelly. Even though they were people who flouted the law, they abided by some sort of code of conduct. Lenny Rowles did not and that frightened everyone.

'Decision time, Gerry,' said Cara. 'Will you come with me?'

'It's not that easy, I told you that. Look, I have to go, we'll talk later.'

He walked over to the window to peer out nervously into the drive.

'What are you looking for?' she asked.

'I'm pretty sure someone is following me. Mind, could be the cops. Blizzard reckons I'm in this up to my neck, I am sure of it.'

'Like you're not?'

'Not sure how much he knows, though.'

'More than he lets on. Danny always said he was a sharp one.'

'Look, are you sure you'll be alright?' asked Brauner, turning back into the room.

'Yes.' She held out a hand. 'Thanks for asking.'

'Just be careful,' he said.

'And you,' she said.

Brauner walked out of the house and into the grey morning. As the photographer edged his car out into the road, pausing to check he was not being observed, DC Fee Ellis squirmed further down into the seat of the unmarked police vehicle parked nearby and glanced over at the detective in the driving seat. Sergeant David Tulley, a stocky man in his mid-thirties, with fleshy cheeks and a shock of tousled black hair, peered out as Brauner's car went past, then straightened up and started the engine.

'Very interesting,' said Ellis.

'Interesting indeed,' said Tulley edging the car out into the street.

* * *

As the detectives' vehicle kept a good distance behind Brauner's car, a weary John Blizzard was sitting three miles away at the upstairs window of an empty first-floor office on the Hafton West Industrial Estate, peering through binoculars at the headquarters of GC Haulage Limited. Sitting next to Blizzard were Wendy Talbot and a male officer, a burly man with short-cropped hair, a strong jaw line, and an effective line in brooding silence.

The building in which they were sitting had been empty since the collapse of an engineering design company four years previously and the floors were covered in dust, the air thick and musty with neglect. The Regional Organised Crime Unit had chosen it for their surveillance because it was possible to see left, through one of the windows, as far as the busy main road leading into the city centre, and right, through another window, the haulage depot. The Unit had been ensconced in the building for the best part of five weeks and the office floor was littered with drinks cans and sandwich wrappings. There was the smell of stale cigarette smoke.

For their part, the three officers had been in the room since midnight when they edged their car, with headlights extinguished, through the narrow alleyway off the main road into the walled car-park behind the building, and walked up the darkened fire escape to relieve the watch. It had proved an eventful night. Just before two, five minutes after the site security van had left the estate following the guard's hourly checks, a lorry had driven off the main road and pulled up outside the depot, its headlights piercing the blackness of the night — most of the estate's street lamps had long been smashed by vandals. Two men had opened the main gates and the lorry had edged its way into the yard and through into the garage. Although the watching detectives did not have a good view of the yard behind the high wall, they could make out enough from the flickering lights to surmise that the men were unloading something.

'Do we go in?' Blizzard had asked; he knew officers were waiting in cars dotted around the area.

'I don't see Cargill,' Talbot had replied, reaching for her flask of coffee and sandwich box. 'We want him as well.'

The lorry departed and the watchers settled down again, Talbot taking the opportunity to elaborate her theories on the death of Danny Galston, still contending that he had fallen foul of gang members who feared he would betray them. Blizzard deliberately said little, offered nothing, but was forced to admit, albeit reluctantly and under pressure, that there was some logic to the theory. Shortly after three, Talbot announced her intention to grab some sleep and silence reigned once more in the dark office, the Regional Organised Crime Unit man staring wordlessly out of the window.

Inevitably, Blizzard's thoughts turned to Keeper, to those children who had suffered in silence for so many years, the reason the officers had risked their careers. Sitting in the darkness, Blizzard sensed he could almost hear children's voices echoing across the sleeping city, like the noise of a distant school playground carried on the wind, the voices faint yet strangely clear, words unformed yet speaking to him all the same. Blizzard's mind went back to the strange little girl in the cemetery. It was as if she was trying to tell him something. She was not a hallucination, he realised with a jolt, but someone dredged deep from within. The doctor had been right: the inquiry was about Pauline Galston, had always been about Pauline Galston. It was about closure and that meant unmasking those who had performed their depravities behind a veil of secrecy for too long. It meant breaking through the terror and intimidation they had created and in some way the death of Danny Galston had started to do that.

'Endgame,' murmured Blizzard, without realising he had said it.

The Regional Organised Crime Unit man glanced over but said nothing. Eventually, Blizzard slipped into uncomfortable sleep for an hour or two as the man kept his lonely vigil. Now, in the grey light of morning, all three were awake and looking expectantly through binoculars at the haulage depot. Shortly after 8.45am, Ralph Cargill arrived in his green Jaguar and a quarter of an hour later, a lorry edged its way out of the main garage, across the yard and out through the depot gates. The watching officers tensed. Once outside the depot, the driver jumped out of his cab and walked back into the yard.

'So, do we go in, ma'am?' asked the Regional Organised Crime Unit man, the first time he had spoken in the best part of three hours.

'I'd rather take it here,' said Talbot. She fished the radio out of her coat pocket. 'All units, stand-by.'

The detectives started to stand up when something made Blizzard glance back towards the main road.

'What the…?' he said.

A small group of people had walked round the corner and were heading solemnly into the industrial estate in the direction of the haulage depot. The officers watched them in bemusement from the office window. At their head was a pale woman in her early fifties, wearing a headscarf, a dun brown jacket and a tweed skirt. Behind her were half a dozen other women, two of whom were pushing buggies containing small children. A couple of the others were pensioners. There were no men.

'Who the hell are they?' asked Talbot.

'Not sure,' said Blizzard.

'Well, why not? You're the sodding local officer.'

Blizzard said nothing but glowered at her – he hated being made to sound like a beat bobby. As the officers watched, the small group walked with slow and deliberate steps past their vantage point, neither looking to left or right. Blizzard noticed that the leading woman was holding a floral wreath and that everyone was wearing dark clothing. Like a funeral, he thought uneasily. But who had died? The group stopped outside the depot, silently blocking the path of the lorry. One of the women glanced at her watch and said something. They all turned to look towards the main road.

Blizzard's radio crackled into life.

'Guv,' said Colley urgently. 'I've just had Fee on. Brauner is heading for your position.'

'Jesus, that's all we need,' exclaimed Talbot. 'This could screw everything up.'

'Like it's not already?' said Blizzard. He glanced at the strange gathering outside the depot, and adding slyly, 'Hey, if Brauner arrives in time, at least you'll get your picture on the front page. Your lot like that sort of thing.'

Talbot scowled. The other Regional Organised Crime Unit officer said nothing. Outside, the women stood in the street for a couple of moments then the detectives followed their gaze to the car that had now edged its way into the industrial estate.

'Brauner,' said Blizzard bleakly.

Watching the photographer walk, camera bag over shoulder, towards the depot, the detectives noticed that the lorry driver had re-emerged from the yard, clutching a sandwich box and coffee flask, and was striding towards his vehicle. Shooting a bemused look at the women, he clambered into his cab, slipped the engine into gear and the lorry started to move forward. The women walked forwards and, holding hands, formed a line blocking the driver's way. The driver honked his horn several times but they refused to move and when he tried to mount the pavement and squeeze past them, two of the women broke off and again stood in his path.

The driver jumped out of his cab and shouted at the women. When they still refused to move, he stormed back into the yard and the group leader glanced at her watch then said something which made the women bow their heads in prayer. As they stood in silence, the leader uttering a few solemn words, Brauner took their photographs then the leader placed her wreath in front of the lorry. As she straightened up, a man in blue overalls ran across the yard towards them.

'Cargill,' said Talbot.

Ralph Cargill marched out of the gates and up to the group and there was a brief confrontation, during which Brauner stepped forward and tried to take a picture. Cargill reacted furiously and snatched out a hand to grab the camera. There was a brief struggle, during which Brauner fell to the floor, dropping his camera.

Brauner clambered to his feet and lashed out a fist, catching Cargill on the side of the face. The depot owner staggered backwards and leaned briefly against the wall then lunged back at Brauner. For a few seconds, the detectives watched transfixed as the two men tumbled backwards and rolled around on the pavement.

'I've had enough of this shite,' snapped Talbot. She lifted the radio to her mouth. 'All units, go!'

As the three officers thundered down the office block stairs, there was a squeal of tyres and four police cars careered onto the industrial estate from the main road and screeched towards the depot, scattering the group of terrified women. Cargill broke off from fighting, yelled at his driver and ran back into the yard, desperately attempting to swing shut the large gates. But he was too late and the lead car slammed into the gates, ripping one of them from its hinges. Two other cars followed it into the yard while the final vehicle blocked the lorry's path. Within seconds, the yard was full of police officers and the air reverberated to the sound of shouting. A couple of the workers tried to escape but were captured after brief struggles. Back on the road, other detectives had grabbed the lorry driver, who was attempting to jump into his cab but was eventually wrestled to the ground.

Blizzard and Talbot ran into the yard to find armed police officers training their weapons on several company employees, who were looking frightened and holding their hands above their heads.

'Where's Cargill?' asked Talbot, whirling round.

There was the sound of breaking glass from inside the office block and several officers sprinted towards the building, kicking in the front door and hurling themselves down the corridor and out of sight. Back in the road, two more cars headed into the industrial estate and flung themselves sideways to block Gerry Brauner's vehicle as the photographer tried to escape the scene. Brauner looked as if he was going to remonstrate with the officers but when Colley got out of one and Ellis and Tulley spilled out of the other, he thought better of it and allowed the DC to restrain him. Colley left Ellis to look after the photographer and walked into the yard.

'Need any help?' he asked, glancing at Blizzard, who was breathing heavily and clutching his aching back.

'No, I think we're OK,' said the chief inspector. He gestured to the ugly gash on the sergeant's forehead. 'You any better?'

'I'm OK. What's happening in there?'

'Cargill's had it away on his toes. Hey, did you pass a group of women on your way in?'

'Yeah, they were walking along the main road.'

'Didn't you think to nick them?'

'For what, walking on the pavement? Besides, we were too busy lifting Gerry Brauner.'

He nodded at Ellis, who had brought the glum-looking photographer to the entrance of the yard.

'Yeah, OK,' said Blizzard. 'Listen, will you get the lads to take a scout round for the women?'

'Will do. Er, why?'

'I have no idea.'

'You'll never get that to stick in court.'

Colley walked off, talking into his radio.

A shout distracted the chief inspector's attention and he ran round to the back of the wagon that was still standing at the depot gates. He looked up at Talbot, who was in the back of the truck, peering at the crates stacked up there.

'I take it they're not vodka?' asked Blizzard.

'Not sure you can drink one of these,' said Talbot, fishing out an assault rifle.

'Bloody hell,' said the chief inspector. He climbed into the wagon and peering into another crate to find more guns. 'There's enough here to start World War Three.'

'There certainly is,' said Talbot, jumping down. 'Sure you don't want to join us?'

'Any sign of Cargill?' asked the chief inspector blandly.

The comment wiped the smile from her face.

'Apparently, he jumped out of the back window and into the canal,' she said. 'But we'll get him.'

'Well, if you don't, the typhoid will.'

Talbot said nothing and started to walk across the yard. After a few paces, she turned.

'Mind, I tell you what,' she said, nodding at the crates. 'If this was the kind of world Danny Galston was involved in, I'd lay odds that one of his associates murdered him.'

'So why not just shoot him?' asked Blizzard, jumping down from the truck. 'Would seem a pity to bring in enough firepower to invade half of Europe then bash his brains out with a rock.'

'Have it your way but when we get him, Cargill is mine first, remember?'

'But of course,' said Blizzard sweetly as she walked towards the office block. 'A promise is a promise.'

His words were to stay with Wendy Talbot for the rest of the day: she recognised the tone only too well and remembered the last time she had used it while talking to him. Blizzard did not follow her. Instead, he stared thoughtfully along the road where the women had performed their ceremony minutes before. The chief inspector glanced at the wreath, which was still lying in front of the lorry and had now attracted the interest of Colley.

'Emily Garbutt, aged eight,' said the sergeant, crouching down to read the dedication on the card and moving some leaves aside to reveal the remainder of the dedication. 'She died in 1981. Hey, today's the anniversary.'

'Now that's interesting. Come on.' Blizzard glanced back at the officers in the yard. 'Let's leave them to it.'

'What about him?' asked the sergeant, straightening up and gesturing to Brauner, who was still being held by Ellis.

'We'll take him back to the station. It's time he answered some questions. Maybe he can tell us who Emily Garbutt was. I have a feeling she's important.'

'Kids, eh?' said Colley.

Chapter nineteen

By nine-thirty, Abbey Road Police Station had been taken over by the Regional Organised Crime Unit. Despite the escape of Ralph Cargill, there was still a sense of triumphalism and officers walked briskly along the corridors, a spring in their step, chests pushed out, the detectives safe in the knowledge that they had arrested key players in an international gun-running gang. Wondering if his negative reaction was because he actually felt jealous, John Blizzard retreated to his office, closing the door firmly behind him. Having been up all night, it was not long before he was asleep.

As he slumbered, Wendy Talbot was giving a press conference in the canteen, revealing to an excited media scrum that raids had also taken place in Leeds during which other members of the gang had been arrested, and that their counterparts in Moscow had moved in on an apartment block. There was, she announced dramatically, an armed siege taking place as she spoke. The media loved it. There was no mention of Ralph Cargill's escape by Talbot but she knew it was only a matter of time before the journalists and camera crews heading back to the industrial estate after the briefing worked out that someone was missing: underwater search teams were already at work in the canal.

Blizzard jerked awake and tried to get on with some paperwork, but after trying to read the same document three times, he sighed, tossed it back onto the desk and sat, his lips pursed as he stared out of the rain-flecked window in the gloom of a Hafton winter's morning. His reverie was interrupted by a knock on the door and in walked Arthur Ronald.

'Not part of the celebrations?' asked the superintendent.

'Forgot my party hat, Arthur.'

'Come on, John,' said Ronald, the chair creaking as he lowered his bulk. 'It's a good result.'

'Yeah, I know.'

'So why the long face?'

'Because I wanted to get Cargill into an interview room and they've let him get away.'

'Perhaps he's not yours to interview. Don't look like that. Wendy is still adamant that Danny Galston was murdered as part of the gun-running and there's plenty can see merit in the idea.'

'She's wrong.' Before Blizzard could elaborate further, there was a knock on the door and in walked Colley. Ronald looked at the sergeant's gashed features with concern.

'Should you be here?' he asked.

'I'm fine, sir.'

'Any ideas who attacked you?' asked Ronald.

'It was too dark to see but he was a big bugger, I'll tell you that.'

'And your informant?'

'Not sure,' said Colley. 'I hope he got away but the guy who attacked me was a real psycho and I reckon he must have known Barry was going to tell me something.'

'What's this about something changing things?'

'Not sure. Maybe there's a link to the guy who did me. Anyway, I came here for something else, actually, and you are not going to like it. Wendy Talbot has just told the press conference that they are linking the death of Danny Galston to the gun-running.'

'I'm sure she has,' said Blizzard.

'You don't seem as pissed off as I thought you would be, guv. Aren't you going to kick the filing cabinet?'

Colley nodded at the cabinet in the corner of the office, the numerous dents in its bodywork testimony to many assaults over the years.

'I'll do it for you if you want,' added the sergeant.

'There's no need,' said Blizzard. 'It takes the focus off us, doesn't it? If everyone thinks we are looking for some gun-toting maniac, we can work nice and quietly without anyone asking any questions. Just the way we like it, boys.'

There was another knock on the door and Tulley entered. As the detective sergeant stood there, he had his usual hangdog appearance and his heavy eyes displayed his weariness following the night's surveillance. Never the sharpest of dressers, Tulley's dark suit was crumpled and the jacket was flecked with crumbs from the Cornish pasty he had purchased from a roadside snack-shack an hour before.

'You look like crap,' said Blizzard.

'Thank you for those few kind words, guv. It makes all my hard work so much more worthwhile. Anyway, sorry to disturb you but they've found a body in the canal, close to the haulage depot.'

'Guess we'll never get to interview Cargill now,' said Blizzard bleakly.

'I wouldn't be so sure about that. See, it's not him.'

* * *

Late that afternoon, an increasingly weary Blizzard and Colley were in the city's general hospital to attend the post-mortem by pathologist Peter Reynolds. A balding middle-aged little man with piggy eyes gleaming out of a chubby face, and dressed in a shabby, ill-fitting black suit, Reynolds knew Blizzard had never liked him and played up to the situation whenever the opportunity arose. Normally Colley would have leaned against a wall and waited for the fun to begin but this time was different. This time the body on the slab was Barry Lawson and the sergeant stood and stared down at it in horror, feelings of guilt washing over him. Barry Lawson had lost his life because of what he had been about to tell Colley and the knowledge troubled him. But it also excited the sergeant, imbuing him with an overwhelming sense that Keeper was finally closing in on the success its members had craved for so many years. The sergeant glanced over at Blizzard, who was watching with increasing irritation as the pathologist examined the body slowly and thoroughly.

'Well?' asked Blizzard impatiently.

'No, he's not,' said Reynolds, without looking up. 'In fact, I'm prepared to hazard a guess that your Mr Lawson is as dead as the proverbial dodo, Blizzard.'

'What killed him? I can't see anything.'

'Which is why you are a humble detective and I am highly-paid and nationally-respected pathologist.'

Despite his sadness at Lawson's death, Colley allowed himself a slight smile and walked over to take his customary position leaning against the wall.

'Just examine the body,' grunted Blizzard.

'I understand he was found in the canal?' said Reynolds.

'Yeah. Some woman walking her dog spotted him floating face down.'

'Not far from the raid this morning, I think.'

'What the hell has that got to do with it?'

'Well, I am just wondering if I should not be reporting to that nice DCI Talbot on this one,' said Reynolds, straightening up, his examination complete. 'I rather got the impression she was doing all your cases these days, Blizzard.'

'She certainly is not!'

Colley failed to restrain the chuckle as he noticed the mischievous twinkle in the pathologist's eye. Blizzard turned and scowled at his friend who mouthed the word 'sorry' and tried to look serious.

'Look,' continued Blizzard, glaring at the pathologist, 'I have had virtually no sleep and I really am not in the mood for your games. All I want to know is how he died.'

'As far as I can see, the cause of Mr Lawson's death was a blow to the back of the head. You can't see it from there, it's under the hairline. Probably happened shortly before he went into the water. Rather reminds me of the injury to Danny Galston, actually.'

'So, are you saying the same person did it?'

'It has always been my opinion that bashing a person's brains out takes very little skill,' said Reynolds, walking over to the sink. 'Indeed, I imagine anyone is capable of doing it.'

'Worth remembering that,' said Blizzard darkly as he headed for the door.

'Hey,' said Reynolds. He turned round from scrubbing his hands. 'If you're finding this all a bit trying, you could always ask that nice Wendy Talbot to take over. I hear she's very good. Came over very well on the television news as well, I thought.'

The detectives could still hear the pathologist's laughter as they walked down the corridor.

* * *

'Barry Lawson is dead,' said Brauner flatly.

Cara looked at him with a shocked expression. It was late-afternoon and he was standing in Cara Galston's living room, surveying the battered and bruised widow. The house had been Brauner's first call after being released by the police and, on arriving, he had made them both tea; even that had seemed beyond Cara as she sat on the sofa twisting and untwisting her necklace with a trembling hand.

'How did he die?' she asked eventually.

'Someone dumped him in the canal. My money's on Rowles. Presumably, Barry could not keep his mouth shut.'

Cara said nothing.

Chapter twenty

'Look, I am not going to back down on this,' said Wendy Talbot. 'It is pointless you looking at me like that, Blizzard. We are going to handle the investigation into the death of Barry Lawson and that is that.'

It was shortly before six that evening and the two officers were sitting in Arthur Ronald's office. It had been a fractious meeting with Ronald struggling to keep order as the two detectives argued vehemently, the atmosphere not helped by Blizzard's foul mood as fatigue took increasing hold of him.

'I'm not backing down either,' he said. 'There is nothing to link Lawson with your gun-runners and you know it.'

'We do not know any such thing at this stage. I mean, he did turn up in the canal near the depot.'

'So did a couple of old boots and a sodding bedstead – you going to arrest them as well?' snapped Blizzard.

'I hardly think that kind of comment is…'

'Please,' said Ronald, holding up a hand. 'Please.'

'Perhaps if you head down to the river, you'll find Ralph Cargill as well,' said Blizzard, ignoring his friend, acutely conscious that he was ranting but too tired to restrain himself. 'Hey, perhaps he's still swimming. Maybe he's reached France by now.'

'For God's sake!' snapped Talbot. 'Ralph Cargill...'

'Ralph Cargill got out of the back of a depot you were supposed to have secured,' said Blizzard. 'And what is more...'

'Alright, that's enough,' said Ronald loudly, glaring at both of them. 'This is getting us nowhere. The only way round this is working together.'

'With all due respect,' said Talbot, 'this is a Regional Organised Crime Unit inquiry.'

'But it's an inquiry in my patch,' said Ronald. 'And what's more, no one had the decency to tell me about it for weeks, if you recall.'

'Yeah,' said Blizzard. 'You can't investigate every bloody crime in this city, you know, Wendy.'

'I'm happy to let CID handle whoever stole your bike,' said Talbot with the merest of smiles.

Blizzard looked at her balefully but said nothing; he was already embarrassed enough that news of the theft had leaked out. Colley, when confronted about it by his friend earlier in the day, had denied telling anyone about the theft and Blizzard now suspected the uniform constable to whom he submitted the formal report. Without any evidence to prove it, the chief inspector had satisfied himself with glowering at the young officer when he passed him in the corridor that afternoon. The PC had grinned, further increasing Blizzard's bad mood.

'So, what are you suggesting, Arthur?' asked Talbot. 'Because I am sure I do not have to remind you that when the Regional Organised Crime Unit come into an area on something like this, we assume the responsibility for handling...'

'You can stop playing politics with me!' snapped Ronald, surprising the others with his vehemence. 'I'm not happy with the way they have behaved over this and the last thing I want is any more half-arsing about.'

'Yes, but…'

'But nothing, Wendy. I hoped I would not have to do this but you leave me no option. I talked to our deputy chief constable an hour or so ago. I think you know him, he used to be a detective over Yorkshire way. In fact, I think I am right in saying he had a stint in the Regional Organised Crime Unit.'

'I know Ken Bright,' said Talbot bleakly. 'Not exactly my favourite person.'

'It seems to be mutual because Ken agreed that you should report to me on this one.'

'Well, do not think for a minute that my chief super will go for any of this.'

'Actually, he did. Did I mention that that he and Ken go back many years? Like I said, Wendy, don't play politics with me.'

Talbot stalked wordlessly from the room, brushing past Colley in the corridor, almost spilling the mugs of tea the sergeant was carrying.

'Is "half-arsing about" an official management term now then?' asked Blizzard.

Ronald allowed himself a grin and Blizzard headed for his office to find Colley, sitting sipping his tea and reading the paper. Colley gestured to a mug on the chief inspector's desk.

'Might be getting a bit cold, mind,' said the sergeant.

'You'll make someone a lovely wife.'

'How did it go with our Wendy? She looked pretty angry. Will the cleaners be able to get the blood off Arthur's wall, do you think?'

'Might take a while,' said Blizzard, sitting down and wincing slightly as his back gave the first twinge in a couple of days. 'Anything new?'

'Certainly is. I have just taken a call from someone at Brian Graham's accountancy firm. Said they can keep silent no longer. Like I always say, follow the money and you can't go far wrong.'

* * *

Half an hour later, the officers were sitting once more in the living room of Brian Graham's plush west end home. It was another gloomy evening and the rain that had been squalling in off the river for much of the day was driving hard against the windows. The accountant was trying not to look worried but his unease showed through in the way he gripped the handle of his coffee mug a little too tightly. Blizzard and Colley exchanged glances and deliberately allowed the silence to lengthen, increasing the tension in the room. It was one of their favourite tricks for unsettling interviewees.

'I see you raided the depot,' said Graham.

'Yes, we did,' said Blizzard.

'Is that why you are here?'

'Actually, no. The sergeant here has unearthed something really interesting. Seems that you have not been telling us everything, Mr Graham.'

'Now hang on a minute, I have been completely honest.'

'I think not,' said the chief inspector. 'It may be time to tell us about Cara Galston's business dealings. Or would you rather the good sergeant enlightens you?'

'I have no idea what you mean.'

'Ah, but I think you have,' said Blizzard. 'You see, when we talked to you last time, you omitted to mention that not only do you do accountancy work for GC Haulage but you also represent the widow Galston.'

'Why on earth should that be relevant? She is just a client who…'

'Who stands to inherit Danny's half of the company, I think. Ten million-plus, if I am not mistaken. Is that not right, Sergeant?'

'And that is a conservative estimate,' said Colley.

'That is confidential information!' exclaimed Graham.

'We tend not to do confidential,' said Blizzard. 'So, is it correct that Cara Galston has already asked you to sell her share of the company, presumably to Ralph Cargill? Perhaps Cara feels the money will help ease the grief of losing her husband in such tragic circumstances. What do you think, Sergeant?'

'Got to help.'

'Who told you about this?' blustered Graham.

'Someone with a damned sight more conscience than you,' snapped Blizzard. 'If Cara has tried to cash in on Danny's death, some souls more cynical than our good selves may describe that as a pretty strong motive to kill her husband.'

Graham looked at him in horror then the fight seemed to go out of him and he slumped back in his chair.

'OK,' he said. 'Yes, Cara does want to sell her share of the company and Ralph has first refusal. It felt wrong when she rang me and asked me to make the approach – Danny had only been dead less than 48 hours – but she was most insistent.'

'So, does Ralph Cargill know about the offer yet?' asked Blizzard.

'I contacted him the same day. It's no secret that Ralph always wanted to own the company. I imagine you're going to call that motive as well, Chief Inspector?'

'Frankly, Mr Graham, I am toying with drawing up a list of people who did not have reason to kill Danny Galston. It would probably be shorter.'

'There were certainly plenty with little reason to like him.'

'Like?'

'Half the hauliers in the city, for a start. I assume you know that GC Haulage was growing rapidly by taking over other companies?'

'We had heard,' said Colley. 'It seems they were very successful in, how can we phrase it, persuading reluctant competitors to sell?'

'Danny and Ralph certainly made plenty of enemies with the way they really screwed them into the ground,' said Graham.

'And if they tried to resist?' asked Blizzard.

'GC Haulage undercut them on contracts until they came crawling back. They were ruthless.' Graham shook his head. 'Absolutely ruthless.'

'We'll need names,' said Blizzard.

After a few more minutes talking, the detectives headed for the door. Brian Graham had a look of intense relief on his face as he ushered them into the hallway.

'There was one more thing,' said the sergeant as Graham opened the front door. 'Does the name Emily Garbutt mean anything? She was an eight-year-old who died in a road accident 15 years ago.'

'I know who she was.'

'And?'

'Perhaps we had better sit down again, gentlemen,' said Graham.

They went back into the living room and Graham went into the kitchen to make a pot of tea. As the detectives sat and listened to the clink of crockery, Blizzard glanced at his sergeant.

'How did you know it would have that kind of effect on him?' asked the chief inspector.

'One of my little hunches.'

The officers looked over to the kitchen door to see Graham emerge with a tray. Once he had sat down in the armchair and poured their cups of tea, the accountant looked at the officers.

'Have either of you got children?' he asked.

Colley shook his head but spotted Blizzard giving him a sideways glance. The sergeant frowned; he had suspected for a while that his friend knew Jay was pregnant.

'Me neither,' said Graham. 'I love kids but Susan couldn't, well, you know... couldn't. It was always a great sadness to us.'

He gazed down at the carpet for a moment.

'I assume you know that the lorry that killed Emily Garbutt was driven by one of GC's drivers,' he said after a few moments.

'Ray Heskey,' said Colley. 'The one whose gravestone was vandalised a few weeks ago.'

'I still see Emily's mother around the city,' said Graham. 'Poor woman. She was absolutely devastated by her daughter's death.'

He stared absently out of the window and silence settled on the room for a few moments.

'This will sound a terrible thing to say,' said Graham after a few moments, 'but whenever I see Janice Garbutt, I say a silent prayer of thanks that I did not have children. I mean, to have to go through that. Does that sound heartless?'

'If you never love, you can never lose,' said Blizzard. 'It seems a sad way to live your life, Mr Graham.'

'Yes, I suppose it is,' murmured the accountant. 'I suppose it is.'

Colley said nothing. Somehow he could not summon the words.

Chapter twenty-one

The little tearoom not far from Abbey Road Police Station was all but deserted when John Blizzard arrived shortly after ten the following morning. Georgia Horwood, looking tired and anxious, was already there, dressed as primly as ever, her bony hand resting on the handle of a mug of tea. She seemed out of place. Georgia looked up as the chief inspector entered.

'Refill?' asked Blizzard.

'No, thank you,' she replied.

She gripped the handle a little tighter as if he was about to snatch it from her. Blizzard walked up to the counter and returned a few moments later, clutching his own mug of steaming tea. Sitting down, he eyed Georgia with interest. She looked nervous and, as ever, there was that sense of secrets untold behind her troubled eyes. That her name had cropped up in their inquiries again was intriguing the chief inspector, but he said nothing for a second or two, preferring to take a sip of tea while he studied her. She looked out of the window, unwilling to meet his gaze.

'Why am I here?' she asked.

'I want to talk about Emily Garbutt.'

'That was 15 years ago.'

'My sergeant came across your name in her case file. You seem to keep cropping up in our inquiries. You were a good friend of Emily's mother, I think.'

'I have not seen Janice for years.'

'But you did know her once?'

She nodded.

'How?' asked Blizzard.

'I ran a playgroup at St Wilfred's Church. Gave me something to do after my husband left me. Janice started bringing Emily.' Georgia smiled at the memory. 'She was a sparky little thing. Full of life. Such a tragedy when... well, I assume you know what happened to her.'

'Yes, we do. When did you stop being friends with Janice? When Emily died?'

'No, before that. Emily went to school and we sort of drifted apart like people do. I often think I should have kept in touch.'

'You are not quite telling me all the story, though, are you? I've read the witness statement from you.'

'I was driving not far behind when it happened. I was on my way to St Wilfred's for the playgroup. Look, is this really relevant, Chief Inspector?'

'Janice Garbutt laid a wreath at GH Haulage yesterday morning, just minutes before the police raid. That makes it relevant, Georgia.'

'How?'

'Few people had a stronger reason to kill Danny Galston than Janice Garbutt. Tell me what happened that day.'

Georgia stared out of the window for a moment or two at the pedestrians scurrying past to the nearby shops and the cars heading towards the nearby roundabout. For a moment, Blizzard wondered if she was going to stand up and walk out of the café but instead she turned back to look at him.

'I shall never forget that day,' she said softly. 'It was foul weather, absolutely foul.'

John Blizzard sat and listened quietly to the story unfolding through Georgia's words, sometimes strong, sometimes quavering, sometimes so quiet the chief inspector had to strain to hear them. As he listened, he was struck, as so often, by the way written statements came to life in the mouths of witnesses. Blizzard found himself forgetting he was in a café as he was transported back 15 years to 9.14am on a rainy day in 1981, Hafton brooding, as so often, beneath dark winter skies. For three days, the city had been living up to its reputation as one of the wettest places in northern England. It had been raining solid without a break and glum-faced pedestrians walking along the main road that morning, past the entrance to Hafton West Industrial Estate, sploshed through large puddles. A steady stream of cars and lorries drove towards the city centre, their paintwork gleaming with the incessant rain and windscreen wipers on full speed to cope with the spray thrown up from the deluged road.

Among the scurrying pedestrians was eight-year-old Emily Garbutt, late for school. She was always late because her mother was so disorganised and morning in their house was always chaotic. It had not always been so. When Emily's father was alive, he left for work at eight and always made sure that his daughter and wife were up and ready when he walked out of the house. But since his death from cancer at the age of 41, the household had descended into chaos and Janice Garbutt, struggling to cope and taking increasing amounts of sleeping pills, found each morning a battle.

Inevitably on the morning of her death, Emily was rushing. Clutching her mother's hand, she hurried along the main road, her hat pulled down around her ears and her knapsack sodden and growing heavier with every step. They were on the wrong side of the main road and needed to cross to reach the primary school in a side street not far from the industrial estate. Realising that, as usual, they had missed the crossing patrol man, they were teetering on the edge of a pavement, waiting for a break in the traffic, when, hidden from their sight round the corner, a lorry rumbled out of the GC Haulage depot, its driver rushing because he was late for the ferry.

Reaching the main road, the driver took a risk and sent his truck lurching into the stream of traffic. Not caring that he had forced other motorists to brake, the driver pushed his pedal to the floor and the lorry juddered and started to gather pace. Ray Heskey was later to tell police that he glanced down and started fiddling with the heater on his dashboard and failed to notice that the car in front of him had slowed to let Janice Garbutt and Emily cross. When he looked up and saw the car's brake-lights, it was too late and the truck was upon the slowing vehicle in a moment. The lorry driver slammed on his own brakes but it was too late and he lost control of his vehicle. The truck veered to its left, clipped the school crossing sign then collided with a garden wall. With the driver battling desperately to regain control, the lorry bounced back onto the carriageway, slammed into a car and ended up embedded in a wall on the other side. When the shaken lorry driver climbed out of his cab, it was to see Emily Garbutt lying motionless in the middle of the road, her sobbing mother cradling her bloodied head.

'I was just behind when it happened,' said Georgia quietly, tears starting to run down her cheeks. 'I ran over to help but the poor little thing had already gone.'

She looked at the chief inspector, who, starting as if shaken awake, nodded and reached for his tea, surprised to discover that it had grown lukewarm during the telling of her story. Time, it seemed, had run on apace without him.

'There's something else I want to ask you about,' he said. 'There's a note in the file that seems to suggest that Janice believes someone else was driving that truck.'

'I am sure there is.'

'I take it you know who she thinks killed her daughter?'

'What comes around goes around,' she said. 'We all have to die sometime.'

'Indeed we do, Georgia,' said Blizzard. 'Indeed we do.'

* * *

That afternoon found Blizzard and Colley at Hafton Cemetery once more. It took a lot to disturb the sergeant but as he and Blizzard stood at the grave of Emily Garbutt, coat collars turned up against the flecks of snow that had started to fall, David Colley's thoughts were in turmoil. The eight-year-old had been buried in a dark corner of the cemetery on the other side from the Galston grave and, as the officers stood silently surveying the picture of a smiling curly-haired child on the gravestone above the words *Safe in the arms of the angels*, the sergeant felt tears welling up. It was the thought of another dead child that had done it. He knew that with children, all the rules changed, that suddenly it became personal for officers working on cases, experiencing as they did a strong sensation that something this terrible should not happen to one so young and innocent. However, on previous cases he had managed to suppress those thoughts with relative ease: the revelation that Jay was pregnant had changed everything for the sergeant. Inevitably, his thoughts turned to the little one yet to be born.

Like Blizzard, the sergeant had vague memories of the tragedy that had befallen Emily Garbutt. Colley had been able to track down the traffic officer that dealt with the case. Recently retired, Charlie Rankin told the sergeant that it was one of the investigations that always rankled with him. Ray Heskey had been charged with careless driving and fined £600, the traffic officer's pleas for a tougher charge rejected by the prosecuting lawyer. Rankin told Colley that, in his opinion, the incident warranted a jail sentence and Colley had agreed. Now, staring at the flecks of snow beginning to settle on the gravestone, the sergeant could not banish the mental image of Emily Garbutt's crumpled body from his mind.

'Penny for them?' asked Blizzard.

'You'll need more than that.'

'Is there something you want to tell me, David?'

Colley shook his head.

'When you're ready, then,' said Blizzard. 'Are you sure mum will be here? On a day like this.'

'Neighbour reckons she never misses.'

'So, what's your view on this? Was Danny Galston driving the truck?'

'Charlie Rankin reckons it's a load of cobblers. I'm tempted to go with his judgement on it.'

'Not sure it matters if Galston was driving or not, does it? As long as Janice Garbutt believes he killed her daughter, it gives her a very strong motive to kill him.'

'Maybe, but like you say, there are plenty of others with strong motives as well. Half the hauliers in this city, for a start, and we should not dismiss Wendy's gun-runners. And Brian Graham seemed pretty angry at the way Danny treated his wife when she was ill.'

The officers stood and stared at the gravestone once again. Neither spoke for a minute or two until Blizzard turned to his colleague.

'So how come Charlie Rankin never mentioned about Danny being the driver?' asked the chief inspector.

'Says he told Harry Roberts.'

'Harry never mentioned it.'

'They both agreed it was rubbish. Filed it away in the NFA drawer.'

'Well it's just come out,' said Blizzard.

Looking round, he saw a middle-aged woman approaching. They both recognised her from the headscarf, which they had seen during the protest the previous morning. She momentarily stopped in her tracks when she saw them standing by her daughter's grave but did not seem surprised.

'I wondered when you would come,' she said, walking towards them.

'Mrs Garbutt,' said Blizzard. 'I think it is time that we had a little chat, don't you?'

He nodded to Colley, who allowed her to place flowers on the grave then led her gently away. Blizzard watched them for a moment or two then looked around, half-expecting to see the strange little girl amid the gravestones, but there was no one there and the cemetery was deserted.

* * *

As the detectives were leaving with their charge, Cara Galston was standing outside their intended destination, Abbey Road Police Station. She took a deep breath and walked up the path, acutely conscious of the thumping of her heart. The news that Barry Lawson had been found floating in the canal had shaken her to the core and she had suddenly found herself overwhelmed with a desire to see the chief inspector immediately. With her plan unravelling around her, and a strong sense that she was in danger, Cara instinctively knew that Blizzard was the only man who could help her carry months of planning to fruition.

She knew further delays could be costly. Barry Lawson's death had come as a terrible shock. No one was supposed to die in the scenario that Cara had rehearsed for several weeks yet now Danny was dead and Lawson was lying on a mortuary slab. Cara had only met Lawson once when he came to their home to see Danny some years previously, the two men disappearing into the kitchen to hold a hurried conversation behind the closed door. Cara had strained to make out the words but remained none the wiser about what brought Lawson to her home. What she did know was that when the two men emerged some minutes later, it was to glance at her with strangely guilty expressions. It was only recently, when Danny told her everything in a drunken moment, that she had been able to fit the pieces of the jigsaw into place.

Hesitating at the police station door, Cara wondered if she was doing the right thing. It had all sounded so easy when she played it through in her mind but now that the moment had come, she was crushed by a sense of import, that things would never be the same once she talked to John Blizzard. Taking another deep breath, she pushed open the door. Cara knew the time had come to tell police and, her mind made up, she walked into the reception area.

'Can I help you, madam?' said the duty officer, looking at her bruised cheek and bandaged hand.

'I would like to see Detective Chief Inspector John Blizzard.'

'I am afraid he is not available. Can I take a message?'

'No.'

She turned to go. Cara was determined that she would only tell Blizzard about her secret. Danny may not have trusted him but there was something about the way Blizzard had looked at her when the detectives told her Danny was dead that convinced her he knew more than he was prepared to let on. Cara hesitated, uncertain as to what to do.

'Can I take a message for Mr Blizzard?' asked the desk sergeant.

'No thanks.'

'Are you in trouble, ma'am? Can I be of assistance?'

'I don't think so.'

'Are you sure? I mean, if you have been assaulted, I can have a female officer talk to you. You look as if you have been the victim of a severe beating there.'

'No, it's alright. I just walked into a door.'

'I've seen those kind of doors before, ma'am. They tend to do it again if you're not careful. Please, if you would just let me help you, perhaps we can...'

'No,' said Cara again, more firmly this time.

She walked hurriedly out of the police station, watched by the officer. He was trying to remember where he had seen her before.

* * *

Half an hour later, Cara Galston was back home, standing looking out of her kitchen window as the rain swept across the garden, spattering on the pond and creating little puddles down by the vegetable patch. As she looked round at her shattered kitchen, her eyes filled with tears and her body was wracked by the sobs that had come so easily over recent days. Amazing as it might have felt to her at one point, she missed Danny, missed the way she felt safe when he was around. He might have had his failings – the anger was with him always – but he was always apologetic after he struck her, always contrite, always in tears.

Cara knew why he lashed out and why he cried. Danny Galston had lived in fear of losing another loved one and each time he struck her, he was gripped by a terror that she would walk out and he would be left alone once more. The couple had never talked about the events of 15 years before, but she had known that the loss of his young family played on his mind more and more with each passing day, bringing with it a deepening sense of guilt at all that had happened. It had made Danny even more determined to protect her. Caring for her was a way of keeping the depression at bay. It was rather sweet, she had always thought.

Then, of course, when she discovered the truth, it all changed. She had listened in mounting horror as it all poured out of his mouth, making terrible sense of his life. Even Cara, a woman who always looked out for number one, had felt revulsion at what she was hearing. However, once she had recovered from her initial shock, her mind began to work out ways in which Danny's misdemeanours might be made to work to her advantage. Lenny Rowles had wrecked all that and, as Cara continued to stare across the window, she instinctively raised a hand to her gashed face. Danny had deserved to die, of that she had no doubt, felt no guilt at believing it, but suddenly, without him, Cara Galston felt more alone than she had ever been in her life.

Chapter twenty-two

'I know what you're thinking,' said Janice Garbutt, eying the detectives calmly, 'but I have not done anything wrong.'

'We never said you had,' replied Blizzard.

It was late afternoon and she was sitting in the interview room at Abbey Road Police Station, the chief inspector and Colley at the other side of the table. Ever since being apprehended, Janice had exhibited little concern about the predicament in which she found herself. Closer inspection of her without the headscarf had revealed a once-handsome woman whose straggly greying hair and lined face told the story of the difficult years she had experienced since the death of her daughter. But the most striking feature was her ice-blue eyes, which now surveyed the detectives keenly, as if she was challenging the detectives to confront her with their suspicions. Here was a woman not disturbed by the situation in which she found herself.

'I would not be here if you did not believe me guilty of something, Chief Inspector,' she said. 'I imagine you think I killed Danny Galston.'

'The thought had crossed our minds. You had more reason than most to hate him.'

'Maybe so, but I did not kill him.'

'His family's gravestone had paint thrown over it,' said Colley. 'I suppose you are going to tell us that that is nothing to do with you either, Mrs Garbutt?'

'Oh, no, I did that, Sergeant. Mea culpa. I did them all.'

The admission, and the casual nature in which it was delivered, stunned the detectives. In the car on the way to the police station, she had maintained a strange calm and the detectives had prepared themselves for a verbal fencing match requiring all their interviewing skills. Her demeanour had led them increasingly to believe that they were dealing with a woman who was hiding secrets and this new turn of events took them aback.

'Would you care to tell us why you attacked the gravestone?' asked Blizzard. 'To many people, there are few more abhorrent crimes than desecrating the memories of the dead.'

'It seemed the only thing left to do. Revenge, Chief Inspector. Revenge.'

'I think you had better explain exactly what has been happening.'

'My doctor said that after Emily died, I suffered a nervous breakdown,' began Janice, her voice exhibiting the first break in her composure, 'I just sat around the house, doing nothing, thinking nothing, being nothing. I would not even go into Emily's room. Could not bear to see her things. Gradually, though, I began to pull myself together and started to think more rationally about what happened on the day of the accident.'

'I think you believe that Ray Heskey was not driving the lorry?' said Colley.

'It took a long time for the idea to form but now I believe that the driver was Danny Galston. According to my doctor, my mind blotted out the events of that day but gradually, over time, they started to come back.'

She paused as the memories of that terrible morning crowded in on her once more; despite her calm exterior, tears were never far away with Janice Garbutt.

'You see,' she said, 'as the lorry came towards us, I had a momentary glimpse of the cab. Just for a fraction of a second but it was enough. There were definitely two men inside it.'

'Are you sure?' asked Blizzard. 'I mean, there was a lot happening and my experience of eyewitnesses is that they tend…'

'I remember every single second of what happened. It is like a film that runs time and time again. I wish I could stop it but I can't. After the lorry struck Emily, I have this vivid recollection that the second man jumped out of the cab and ran back towards the industrial estate.'

'Yes, but he could have been the passenger. Ray Heskey could still have been the driver.'

'That's what your PC Rankin said, Chief Inspector. However, there is no doubt in my mind that the man jumped out of the driver's side. I accept that by the time the police arrived, Ray Heskey was the only one in the lorry, but I believe he was told to stay there and take the consequences of the other man's actions.'

'But…' began Blizzard.

'And Ray Heskey was in no position to resist because he had run up considerable debts on the horses. All Galston had to do was threaten to sack him and he would have done anything.'

'But surely the company had several drivers,' said Colley. 'Perhaps it was one of the others?'

'They had eight at the time but one of them was off on long-term leave with a back injury and the rest were out on deliveries elsewhere.'

'So why are you so convinced that it was Danny Galston?'

'Because whoever it was had the power to order Ray Heskey to remain in the cab. Only two people could do that – Danny Galston and Ralph Cargill.'

'So why not Ralph?' asked Blizzard.

'He was bringing a load back from Germany. Danny was the only one left.'

'You seem to have done a lot of research,' said Blizzard.

'I have and I am right.'

'But PC Rankin checked all of this out,' said Colley. 'There was nothing at all to support what you are saying. Not a shred of evidence.'

'Danny Galston was guilty of killing Emily. Of that I am in no doubt and as far your PC Rankin is concerned, I would not exactly say he conducted a thorough investigation. He'd made his mind up right from the start. Danny realised that I knew what he had done. Whenever I saw him in the street in the years that followed, he always averted his gaze.'

'But why throw the paint over the Galston family's gravestone?' asked Blizzard. 'I mean, this all happened 15 years ago.'

'And you think the pain dims?'

'No. No, of course not, but why not do it when you decided that Danny had killed your daughter. Why wait?'

'I did it because of what happened a few weeks ago.'

'Which was?'

'Because of my legal action against CG Haulage.'

'Which is why you know so much about the company, presumably,' said Colley.

'Indeed so. You see, about five years ago, when I realised what Danny had done and the way the company had covered things up, I consulted a lawyer. As time went on, I had become more and more angry about what happened and I wanted to secure justice for Emily.'

'And money for yourself,' said the chief inspector.

'I appreciate that your job is to see the worst in everybody but please believe me when I say money was not what motivated me. If you ask my lawyer, she will tell you that I had already committed in writing to donate all the compensation to St Margaret's Children's Hospice, in Burniston. Emily would have appreciated that, I think. Her father died there. It seemed somehow appropriate.'

Blizzard nodded without realising he had done it. Harry Roberts had died in the same hospice and the chief inspector himself had made several donations down the years. Despite his suspicion about Janice Garbutt, he felt his attitude towards her softening slightly.

'So, have you been paid any compensation?' asked Colley.

'No. Three months ago, my lawyer recommended that I give up my fight. GC Haulage had used every delaying tactic in the book down the years and it was starting to cost too much. My lawyer is a good woman but she could not keep working for free, nor would I expect her to. She said that there was no way the company was ever going to pay up so I abandoned my legal action. I had no options left, really.'

'So you threw paint over the stones in revenge?' asked Blizzard.

'Yes, I did. I was so angry. In fact, I would love you to charge me with criminal damage because then I can say all this in court.'

'But why attack Susan Graham's stone first?' asked Colley. 'Was it simply a case of targeting anyone who worked for the company?'

'She was a bitch.'

'All we know is that she died of cancer,' said Blizzard.

'Just because you die of cancer, that does not mean automatically you are a good human being, Chief Inspector. My husband was a wonderful man but Susan Graham deserved everything she got.'

The detectives looked at her, startled once more by her anger.

'What exactly do you have against her?' asked Blizzard.

'As company secretary, Susan Graham was the one who advised their lawyers. It was down to her that the company never paid compensation. When I heard she had died, I was glad and I don't care who knows it. People like that do not deserve to live.'

'And Ray Heskey?' asked Blizzard. 'Why attack his stone if you did not think he was driving the lorry that killed your daughter? I thought you said he had no option about lying.'

'Everyone has options, Chief Inspector. Ray Heskey had choices but he refused to help Emily which makes him just as guilty as Danny Galston. He was the one who covered it up for all those years. Besides, to have him and the Graham woman both lying in the same cemetery as my poor Emily had always seemed so obscene. Attacking their stones seemed the right thing to do.'

Blizzard nodded. Somehow he found himself agreeing with her.

'And I think we can understand why you attacked the Galston gravestone,' said Colley.

'Actually, I was not going to do it at all,' said Janice. 'Little Chloe wasn't that much younger than Emily and the last thing I wanted to do was deface her memory. I had no argument with her or her mother.'

'So, what made you change your mind?' asked Blizzard.

'Danny Galston rang me one night. Said he knew that I was attacking the stones. Threatened me if I did it again. Said he'd send some people round.'

'So you attacked his stone as well?'

'You were there when I did it, I think, Chief Inspector.'

'How do you know that?' asked Blizzard.

'The old lady who stole the flowers from the crematorium?'

'Yes?' said Blizzard, his mind going back to that afternoon in Hafton Cemetery. Suddenly he remembered the woman in the headscarf.

'I was watching her as well. I've seen her do it before. Quite a turn of speed for a wrinkly, don't you think? I see her in the supermarket sometimes. Steals frozen chickens from them.'

Despite the tension in the room, the detectives smiled at the image of the light-fingered pensioner.

'Tell me,' said Blizzard, after a few moments. 'What is your connection with Gerry Brauner. How come he was at the depot yesterday morning?'

'A friend put me on to him. We did not dare say anything publicly during the legal action – the company would have used it against us – but when it failed, I felt we should do something to draw attention to the case. Gerry said the anniversary was a good opportunity, that the nationals might go for it. Said the papers love what he called 'a dead kid'. Somewhat distasteful, I am sure you will agree, but he might be right. However, we seem to have stumbled upon something. I've never seen so many police officers. The radio said it was about guns. Was CG Haulage smuggling?'

'It's not our investigation,' said Blizzard blandly.

'No, it was that lady called Talbot, I think. She came over very well on the television.'

'Be that as it may,' said the chief inspector, 'whoever murdered Danny Galston is very much my investigation.'

'I freely admit to attacking his family's gravestone, but murdering him? I think not.' Janice sat back and crossed her arms. 'You'll just have to believe me on that one, gentlemen.'

'Yes, I suppose we will,' said Blizzard with a sigh.

The chief inspector nodded to Colley and the sergeant escorted Janice down the corridor to reception. It was as she was about to leave the police station that Janice looked at the detective.

'Have you got children, Sergeant?'

'My partner is pregnant,' said Colley, surprised that of all the people in the world he should choose to divulge the news to Janice Garbutt.

'Well, when the little one arrives, take good care. It can be a dangerous world for children.'

Janice Garbutt walked out of the front doors. The sergeant thought about running after her but something stopped him. As he stood and watched her disappear into the misty evening, he felt cold. The sergeant tried to tell himself it was caused by the chill of the evening but he knew it was something more. When he went back to tell the chief inspector what she had said, Blizzard's office was in darkness and his coat had gone.

Chapter twenty-three

Shortly after ten that evening, Colley picked his way across the expanse of wasteland behind the city centre railway station, heading for an old corrugated shed, the place to which he knew Blizzard retreated when he needed to do some hard thinking. Childhood passion reaching deep into adulthood, Blizzard was one of the founders of the Hafton Railway Appreciation Society, a small group of volunteers who restored steam locomotives. Most of them were retired railmen and the shed was the home of their prize possession, the Silver Flyer. For many years, she had hauled carriages between Hafton and the Midlands, until taken out of commission in the 1960s. Blizzard stumbled across her while investigating an assault that took place on the wasteland and now, the society having raised the money to buy her, he spent as much of his spare time as possible working on the engine.

The sergeant approached the shed, his feet crunching on broken glass. Noticing a light filtering through chinks in the shed door, Colley stood for a moment, his heart pounding and his mouth dry. The sergeant took a deep breath, wrenched open the door, which groaned in protest on rusty hinges, and peered into the half-light provided by a couple of old table lamps balancing precariously on rickety tables. Blizzard was hard at work on the locomotive, crouched in oil-stained blue overalls, his hands gloved against the biting chill.

'Evening, David,' he said, without looking up from the obdurate bolt with which he was battling. 'Must be important to bring you down here at this hour.'

'It is.'

There were a few moment's quiet, the only noise the scraping and scratching of the chief inspector's spanner. Eventually, Blizzard gave a triumphant grunt as the nut came free. Noting the sergeant's uneasy expression, the chief inspector dug out a stool from the mess and placed it next to a ramshackle little table bearing a kettle, a few mugs, a box of teabags and sheaves of paper on which were scrawled instructions for the engineering team.

'So, what's up?' asked Blizzard, gesturing for the sergeant to sit down.

'I'm finding this investigation very difficult.'

'Going to tell me why?' asked Blizzard.

He took the kettle over to the grubby sink in the corner of the workshop.

'I have to tell you that Jay is pregnant,' said Colley.

'I have to tell you? What sort of talk is that? You make it sound like a press conference.'

Blizzard filled the kettle then returned to plug it in and rooted round for another stool.

'Besides, I know she's pregnant.'

'You do?'

'Fee worked it out.'

'How?'

'Dunno. Women know these things. How many weeks is Jay?' The chief inspector smiled at Colley. 'Fee said that was the kind of question to ask about pregnant women. Impressive, eh?'

'Yeah. Twelve weeks.'

'That's the last time I let you go on sodding holiday. Hey, don't look so worried, it's a joke. We are both delighted for you. *I* am delighted for you.'

'Really?'

'Yeah. Besides, Fee is talking about us having one,' said Blizzard. 'Says I'm not getting any younger. Something about a spring chicken.'

Colley chuckled.

'She's got it all mapped out, David,' said the chief inspector. He gave a shake of the head. 'Buy a house in the spring, get married the year after, baby the year after, mow the lawn on a Saturday, wash the car on a bloody Sunday. Even wants me to get a B&Q discount card. I mean, how crap is that?'

'You a dad?' said the sergeant.

'Me with a B&Q card.' Blizzard grinned, then pretended to look affronted. 'Anyway, I would make an excellent father.'

'But you hate kids!'

'Yeah,' said Blizzard. He lowered his voice. 'But I haven't told Fee. I'm waiting for my moment.'

'I think she must have worked it out by now. Bloody hell, who would have believed it?'

'Yeah, well I don't want it spread round the station, Fee would kill me. But having a baby is a happy occasion, surely. Why do you look so worried?'

'It's a lot of responsibility.'

'I reckon that's only half of it,' said Blizzard. He dropped a couple of teabags into the chipped old maroon pot. 'There's been something on your mind for a while.'

'I didn't think you'd noticed.'

'I always notice, David.' Blizzard touched him lightly on the hand, the first time the sergeant could recall him ever doing anything like that. 'Go on, spit it out.'

'Well, I got to thinking it would be nice to bring a kid up away from Hafton. Maybe live abroad. Run a bar, perhaps.'

'Why on earth would you want to run a bar?'

'It doesn't have to be a bar. I mean, what is there here for a kid? You see how many crimes we investigate and there's more and more schoolkids carrying knives and drug dealers on every corner and there's all those murders and...'

'Most people never see a murder,' said Blizzard. He hunted around under the debris on the table for the bottle of milk as the kettle started to groan and wheeze. 'Or get involved in anything worse than being pulled over for speeding. And the only knife they ever see is the one they carve the Sunday joint with. You know that, David.'

'Yes, but what about Chloe Galston? And Pauline? And Emily Garbutt? And what about all the kids in Keeper?'

'What about all the hundreds and thousands of kids who are sleeping safe and peaceful in their beds tonight. Come on, David, you know what the job does to us. We spend all day bumping heads with low-lifes and it turns us a little bit crazy. Why do you think the child protection teams only do six months?'

'Yes, but...'

'You talk to Jay. She spends all day looking at smiling little faces and reading story books about princesses and cheerful dragons. I imagine Jay is not in despair at the state of the world.'

'Maybe.'

'Remember Reg Kirkup? Nicked a burglar then spotted him walking on his estate with his pit-bull so he moved house. Then what happened?'

'As I recall, another burglar walked past his new house the day he moved in. Even looked in some of the boxes.'

'Exactly. Even if he lived on top of a mountain, Charlie would still see a burglar one day.' Blizzard hunted for a couple of mugs on the table. 'Even if he wasn't there. You've read all that fear-of-crime stuff Arthur keeps dumping on my desk. It's part of life. What's important is how you deal with it.'

'OK, but I do feel that…'

'Take my advice, don't do anything hasty. Crack open a bottle of wine and talk to Jay. But remember, the force can't afford to lose officers like you and I sure as hell can't.'

'Thanks for that,' said Colley. 'It's just… I don't know… like sometimes I wish this baby would never be born.'

'Hey,' said Blizzard. He looked at him sharply. 'I don't want to hear talk like that. The baby will be the most brilliant thing that has ever happened to you.'

Colley looked at his friend, marvelling at that rarest of rare sights, a beam on John Blizzard's face, and grinned.

'Yeah,' said the sergeant. 'You might just be right.'

'As always. Was that what you came down here for?'

'There was something else.'

'Don't tell me it's quads?'

'God forbid! No, when I saw Janice Garbutt off this evening, I kinda got the feeling she was trying to tell me something. Said it was a dangerous world for children.'

'Yeah, but her daughter was run over by a truck.'

'I'm sure she was trying to tell me something else. Couldn't get out of the building fast enough when I asked her to explain.'

'I tell you, there's too many people holding out on us,' said Blizzard. He flicked the boiling kettle off and poured the water into the teapot. 'Let's reconvene tomorrow morning, go through the evidence then lift some bodies. Cara Galston, Gerry Brauner. Anyone else we fancy. Janice Garbutt again maybe.'

Colley nodded, delighted to be contemplating police business rather than embarrassing and deeply personal feelings, but before the sergeant could say anything, Blizzard's mobile telephone rang and the chief inspector walked over to his jacket, which was hanging on a peg on the shed door.

'That will be my beloved,' said Blizzard ruefully. 'Telling me my dinner's cold. I haven't been home.'

'Or the bed's hot,' said Colley. He started to pour the tea. 'It's all about temperature, this baby lark, you know. I tell you, it's been a real eye-opener. All you want to do is roll over and go to sleep after a hard day at work and the missus whips out the thermometer and...'

'Yes, thank you, Sergeant,' said Blizzard quickly, locating the mobile and lifting it to his ear.

It was short conversation.

'Who was it?' asked Colley when the chief inspector had finished talking.

'Randall. He's coming over. Says it's important.'

* * *

The shed door gave another groan of protest and in walked a grim-faced Max Randall followed by an equally sombre Alex Mather.

'What's up?' asked Blizzard. 'You look like you've seen a ghost.'

'Maybe we have,' said Randall. 'Alex has heard something.'

'Lenny Rowles is back,' said Mather.

Blizzard said nothing but walked over to the locomotive, absent-mindedly running a hand down her boiler as the thoughts raced through his mind. When he told Fee about the moment the following morning, after a night he would never forget, Blizzard described it as time standing still for a few seconds as old memories came rushing back, memories he had hoped were gone forever, memories of the only man whose propensity for extreme violence had ever truly frightened the chief inspector. Blizzard's mind was crowded with images of the bull-faced Lenny Rowles and his grotesquely damaged victims, dark thoughts of inquiries thwarted time and time again because none of Rowles' cowed victims ever dared give evidence against him.

'Tell me you are kidding, Alex,' said Blizzard.

'I'm not famed for my sense of humour.'

'I reckon it's true,' said Randall. 'There's a lot of frightened people around at the moment. I thought it was something to do with Danny Galston's death but the return of Rowles would explain everything.'

'But why is he back?' asked Colley, who had been equally shaken by the news. 'And what do we do?'

'Well, for a start...' began Blizzard.

Again his phone rang and he walked briskly over to his jacket, fished the device out and placed it to his ear.

'John,' said the desk sergeant at Abbey Road, calling from home having suddenly recalled the visit of the battered blonde to reception earlier in the day. 'I have a major apology to make.'

'For what, George?'

'I was going to tell you earlier then got embroiled in other things and clean forgot. There was a woman in to see you this afternoon.'

'What woman?'

'Attractive blonde piece. Didn't give her name but she had been done over real bad. Domestic, I reckon. I asked her for some details but she said she would only talk to you. Walked out without giving me her name.'

'Sounds like Cara Galston,' said Blizzard.

'Danny's old lady?' said the desk officer with a low whistle. 'Jesus, I thought she looked familiar. Just couldn't place her. Sorry I didn't let you know earlier, old son. Silly mistake.'

'Don't beat yourself up about it, George. And thanks for letting me know.'

Blizzard put the phone away and struggled into his jacket, wincing with the pain as his back protested after its hours in the chill of the engine shed.

'Someone has beaten up Cara Galston,' he said, nodding at Colley. 'We'll go and ask her who did it.'

'We'll fish round for a bit more on Rowles,' said Randall.

'There's a pub I know,' said Mather. 'Maybe I can pick up something there.'

'Be careful, you know what he's like,' said Blizzard.

Mather flapped a hand lazily as he and Randall walked out into the crisp, starlit night. Five minutes later, having put his tools away and made sure the shed was secure, Blizzard headed for the door.

'Come on, Sergeant,' said Blizzard. He clapped his friend on the shoulder. 'Hot bed or not, we've got work to do.'

'Don't we always,' said Colley.

Blizzard padlocked the shed door and, as they walked across the wasteland towards the nearby lights of the city centre, the sergeant's phone rang.

'David,' said the urgent voice of Sergeant Tulley at the other end. 'Gerry Brauner's been spotted near Cara Galston's house and it looks like he's been done over badly.'

'On our way,' said Colley.

Chapter twenty-four

Cara Galston started as the doorbell rang shortly after ten. Heart beating faster and head pounding, she walked on trembling legs into the hallway and to the front door, peering out into the darkness through the fish-eye then crying out in horror. Wrenching off the chain, which she had installed after the attack, she opened the door and Gerry Brauner stumbled into the house, his face covered in blood, one eye closed and his leather jacket ripped and torn.

'My God!' she cried, crouching down as he sank to his knees on the doormat. 'What happened?'

Brauner slumped on the floor, blood seeping out over Cara's tasteful pale blue carpet. Twenty minutes later, he found himself lying on her sofa, a damp flannel placed gently over the worst of his facial gashes and with one eye still partially closed. There was a roaring sound in his ears and, for a few moments, he was not quite sure where he was.

'Here, drink this,' said Cara, kneeling down and handing him a glass of brandy. 'It'll make you feel better.'

'I couldn't feel worse,' he groaned.

'What happened?'

'I'd gone back to the office,' said Brauner, struggling to form the words through swollen lips. 'As I left, these two guys appeared.'

'Was one of them Lenny Rowles?'

There was fear in her voice; Brauner's face provided the answer she had dreaded.

'They tried to get me into their car but I managed to get away but not before I got this little lot.' He winced as he dabbed his nose with the flannel then gave her an accusing look. 'They said something about you going to the police. Please don't tell me that is true, Cara.'

Cara hesitated.

'Well?' he demanded, finding new strength as he sat up.

'I told you I would.'

'Yes, but I never thought you would go through with it!'

'They deserve what they get. Besides, I told you, with Ralph behind bars, I get the company. I've already got a buyer lined up. He's offering £35m – do you know what I can do with that kind of money? And my offer still stands, Gerry, nothing has changed. Nothing.'

'Except you'll get us killed,' exclaimed Brauner, struggling to his feet. 'You've seen what they can do. Next time we won't be so lucky.'

'Calm down – Blizzard wasn't in. I didn't get to speak to him.'

'So what! Once they saw you at the police station…'

'No one saw me, Gerry. Relax.'

'Relax! Relax!' screeched Brauner, hobbling over to thrust his face close to hers so that she could see the blood glistening. 'How can I relax, Cara? They know you were there! They'll come after you as well.'

'Even if they do, it'll be too late.'

'What do you mean?'

'I've made my mind up.' She gestured to a suitcase standing in the corner of the room. 'I'm going. You can come, too. Just like we said. I'll pack a bag with some of Danny's things. But you'll have to be quick. The taxi's due soon.'

'I'm not so sure.' Brauner's voice was small, like a little boy lost.

'Up to you. I'm flying to Spain tomorrow morning. I've got friends there. I can get you on last minute, I am sure. Georgia's going with me as well. I'm picking her up on the way round.'

'I thought she didn't want to go through with it.'

'That was before she realised what they would do to her once they realised I had gone.'

Brauner still hesitated.

'Your decision, Gerry,' she said. 'Always has been.'

'But I can't just up sticks, Cara! Not just like that. What would they do to my wife and kids?'

'Stay and they'll kill you.'

'And what about Blizzard? He'll come after us.'

'Not sure he will.' She fished in her jacket pocket and produced an envelope. 'It's all in here. I'm going to mail it on the way round. By the time he gets it, I'll be out of the country. He'll never find us.'

'Jesus, you've got it all planned out.'

'I told you I had, Gerry. Perhaps you should have listened.' Cara looked across to the window as headlights flashed in the drive. 'Ah, here's the taxi. Decision-time, Gerry.'

Brauner hobbled over to the front window and peeped through the curtains.

'Something's not right,' he said, turning back into the room. 'That's no taxi.'

Cara looked at him in horror as they heard heavy feet on the gravel. Moving swiftly, she slipped the envelope behind the living room radiator. There was a rending sound as the front door was kicked in and two men burst into the room. Brauner recognised them as his attackers earlier that evening and his attention was drawn, now as then, to Lenny Rowles, a large bull-faced man with a shorn head and eyes that seemed to blaze as he surveyed them balefully. He was wearing a black T-shirt which hardly contained his bulging muscles, his arms were heavily tattooed, and his jeans were spattered with Gerry Brauner's blood. Cara went pale as she saw once more the man who had assaulted her in the kitchen.

'Well, well,' rasped Rowles. He glanced at his accomplice, a lean man with slicked-down black hair and a scar on his cheek. 'Two for the price of one.'

His accomplice laughed drily.

'You,' rasped Rowles, pointing at Cara, 'were at the police station!'

She swallowed hard and glanced around the room in a desperate search for a weapon.

'Going somewhere?' asked the other man, noticing the suitcase.

'You ain't going anywhere,' said Rowles. He reached into his jeans pocket and produced a knife. 'I'm going to enjoy this. Should have done it last time. Time to join little Chloe.'

'For God's sake, Lenny,' blurted out Brauner.

Rowles held the knife up and took a step towards the photographer.

'You first then,' he said with a wicked glint in his eye.

Brauner lurched forwards, raising his fists. Rowles lashed out an arm, catching the photographer full on the face. Brauner grunted, staggered backwards and crashed into the sideboard, sending a vase smashing onto the floor. Cara, who had seemed transfixed, regained her senses, screamed and ran into the kitchen. The other man ran after her but as he burst through the door, he saw Cara rummaging frantically through the cutlery draw and turning, clutching a meat knife in her hand.

'One more step!' she screamed.

He hesitated but the sound of Brauner screaming from the living room distracted Cara. It was all the man needed and he snatched the knife and manhandled his struggling prey back into the living-room where Rowles was standing over the crumpled figure of Gerry Brauner, who was groaning and coughing up blood. It was at that moment that Sergeant Dave Tulley and fellow surveillance officer Detective Constable Alan Hayes burst into the room.

'Police!' shouted Tulley.

The intruders seemed rooted to the spot for a moment then, with a savage cry, Rowles lashed out at Tulley, sending him crashing backwards to strike his head against the wall. His accomplice threw Cara roughly to one side and advanced on Hayes, snapping out a fist that caught the officer on the side of the face, sending him backwards to tip over the armchair nearest the front window and lie motionless on the floor. There was a sound from the kitchen and the intruders whirled round as they realised that Cara and Brauner had taken advantage of the fracas and escaped out of the back door, the dazed Brauner hobbling badly, bleeding profusely and leaning heavily on her shoulder. It was as the intruders started to follow, that Tulley staggered to his feet and stumbled forwards. With an enraged bellow, Rowles lunged once again, catching the sergeant on the chin and sending him backwards to hit the wall for a second time, this time to slump to the floor to lie still, blood seeping from his nose.

'You've killed him, you daft bastard!' yelled the villain.

'Not yet!' snarled Rowles.

He aimed a ferocious kick at the motionless sergeant, catching him full in the face.

'Forget him, Lenny!' snapped the man as Rowles turned on the stricken Alan Hayes, who was on his knees by the sofa, coughing up blood.

For a moment, it looked as if Rowles was going to argue but his accomplice grabbed him by the shoulder and gestured to the kitchen. The two intruders dived out into the back garden, looking around wildly, but Cara Galston and Gerry Brauner had disappeared into the night, the photographer somehow dragging his battered and broken body over the fence and dropping into the cul-de-sac behind the house. The assailants raced back through the living room and out through the front door, narrowly missing the taxi pulling up in front of the house. The startled driver slewed his vehicle to one side, smashing into the side of the Galstons' Jaguar. The cabbie staggered out, clutching his hand to a gaping head wound and began to remonstrate with the men but with a furious roar, Rowles lashed out a fist, knocking the driver off his feet and sending him flying through the air to hit the garage door. The driver twitched then lay still. Silence returned to Cara Galston's house. Outside, having staggered through the front door in a desperate attempt to stop the intruders, Alan Hayes slumped to the ground and lay there, eyes closed, head thumping, a sick feeling welling in his stomach. As he slipped in and out of consciousness, he was vaguely aware of the wailing of sirens drifting on the night air.

* * *

Fifteen minutes later, Blizzard and Colley surveyed the scene grimly. Two ambulances were parked in the drive and the badly shaken cabbie was being tended to by a paramedic trying to stop the blood pouring from his facial wound. Another was working on Alan Hayes, who was sitting on a large stone in the front garden wall, his eyes glazed and blood dripping from an ugly gash on his cheek.

Glancing back through the front window of the house, Blizzard could see paramedics lifting Tulley onto a stretcher, having won the first desperate battle to stabilise him. The grim-faced crew emerged with a stretcher on which lay the motionless figure of the sergeant, the scene watched in silence by the small knot of officers that gathered in front of the house. Blizzard walked over and looked down at the battered face of the detective.

'Will he be alright?' he asked hoarsely.

'Too early to say,' said the ambulance man. 'I've never seen anything like this. Such savagery.'

Blizzard nodded and watched them load the stretcher into the ambulance. As the second crew helped the cabbie into the back of the other vehicle then turned back for the limping Alan Hayes, the chief inspector walked over and placed a hand gently on the detective constable's shoulder.

'You alright?' he asked.

'It was Lenny Rowles,' mumbled Hayes.

'I know. Did he say...?'

'Sorry, mate,' said the medic to Blizzard as Hayes stumbled, his knees buckling. 'You'll have to talk to him later.'

Blizzard nodded and watched the ambulanceman help Hayes into the vehicle. The chief inspector turned to Colley.

'So, Mather was right,' said Blizzard. 'Lenny Rowles is not dead.'

'It would appear not.'

The detectives watched the ambulances head off into the night, their blue lights flashing, then looked back at the house. More headlights pierced the night and another car pulled up the drive. The detectives turned to watch Arthur Ronald get out and lumber over to them, his face drawn and anxious.

'Will they be alright?' he asked.

'Not sure about Tulley,' said Blizzard. 'Hayesy should be OK.'

'Rowles?'

Blizzard nodded.

'So, what's our next move?' asked Ronald.

Blizzard glanced back at the house, his face hard set.

'We end it,' he said, 'and we end it right now.'

* * *

Shortly after 1am, with Ronald having gone home and Colley at the hospital, Blizzard was standing alone in Cara Galston's living room, staring out of the front window at the police cars parked on the drive, wrapped up in his own thoughts and impervious to the sounds of forensic officers at work upstairs; they had been searching the house for the best part of two hours. Blizzard had found himself profoundly shocked by the sight of his detectives being taken away to hospital, particularly the motionless figure of Tulley. The inspector had seen many police officers injured in his time but this incident was different and he knew the reason: the re-emergence of Lenny Rowles.

The chief inspector had first encountered Rowles as a young thug but all attempts to bring him to trial foundered because witnesses did not dare give evidence against him. His propensity to use violence in the service of one of the city's major crime families had earned him some powerful protection, but when Rowles was in his early twenties his luck ran out in a bungled robbery when a security van guard was shot in the leg. Blizzard played a central role in the investigation which led to the arrest of three of the raiders but the fourth remained at large. Blizzard became convinced that it was Rowles, but he had vanished. Reports down the years put him everywhere from Spain to Bolivia and, as the years passed, so the stories faded and police began to suspect that he was dead. Now, all that had changed.

Blizzard's gloomy reverie as he stared out of the living room window was disturbed by the return of Colley from the hospital, his car edging its way up the drive, the headlights dazzling the watching chief inspector. Moments later, the sergeant walked into the living room.

'How are they?' asked Blizzard.

'Tulley's still unconscious. Hayesy's got a broken jaw and three busted ribs.'

'And the cabbie?'

'Not too grand. If this was Rowles, he's a bloody animal.'

'He always was,' said Blizzard.

He turned as Max Randall walked into the room.

'I just heard,' said Randall. 'Thought I'd come over and see if you need a hand. I know Lenny Rowles of old. You sure it's him?'

He looked at the blood smeared up the walls.

'It's him,' Randall said.

The detectives heard someone coming down the stairs. Seconds later, forensics chief Graham Ross entered the room.

'Anything?' asked Blizzard hopefully.

'Archie reckons the attackers were wearing gloves. There aren't any good fingerprints. I'll do a double check in here before I go.'

'If it was Rowles, what's the connection with Cara Galston?' asked Randall.

'We always assumed Rowles left Hafton because of the robbery,' said Blizzard. 'What if he also killed Jenny and the kids?'

'But why go for Cara?'

'Unless he was really after Brauner. He was here as well.'

'Guv,' said Ross.

They turned to see him reach behind the radiator and pull out the envelope that Cara had hurriedly concealed.

'It's addressed to you,' said the forensics officer.

Blizzard opened it and read the contents swiftly, his eyes widening as he did so.

He handed the letter to Randall.

'End-game,' he said.

Chapter twenty-five

Shortly after ten o'clock the next morning, a tired John Blizzard walked slowly along one of the paths in Hafton Cemetery, heading for the grave of Emily Garbutt. He had spent a lot of time at the cemetery over recent weeks: normally he visited a couple of times a month. Whenever he came, he was struck by the way the cemetery provided sanctuary from the pressures of the world outside: Blizzard had often told Colley that he had a greater affinity with the dead than the living. It was one of his favourite sayings. He also liked the idea that he could turn off his mobile phone and not feel guilty about it.

On his visits, the chief inspector liked to wander between the graves, reading the inscriptions on the stones and wondering at the lives lived by those people. Sometimes, he found himself standing rapt in thought, impervious to the passage of time, as certain inscriptions told stories so unbelievably poignant that it was difficult to bear. For all the sadness, there had always been a sense of peace in Hafton Cemetery and the chief inspector liked that. But the appearance of the strange little girl followed so quickly by the murder of Danny Galston had changed all that and imbued the cemetery with a different atmosphere. So it was with heavy foot that John Blizzard walked towards the grave, overwhelmed by a feeling that the cemetery was about to give up one of its darkest secrets.

As he rounded the corner, he saw, as he had expected, Emily's mother standing in the morning mist, having just placed flowers at her daughter's final resting place. The chief inspector stopped and surveyed her for a moment or two. He knew that the flowers on the grave were always fresh, that it was a part of the ritual that kept Janice Garbutt's fragile facade together, and it was such a deeply personal scene that part of the chief inspector dearly wished he could turn and leave and not intrude on such precious memories. But John Blizzard knew that the cemetery's serenity had been shattered by events of the past few days and that his job was about to intrude on a peaceful scene that masked dark waters running deep. Cara Galston's letter had confirmed that. Blizzard started reluctantly to walk forward again. Sensing his presence, Janice turned round.

'I thought I might see you here,' she said, with a half-smile. 'I heard about your officers on the radio. How are they?'

'They'll be OK. I take it you know who attacked them?'

'I imagine it was Lenny Rowles.'

'And how exactly do you know that?'

'He's the one who beat Cara up. That is why she was planning to leave Hafton.'

'Well, she is missing,' said Blizzard. 'As is Gerry Brauner. And what's more, we cannot track down Georgia Horwood either.'

'They asked her go with them.'

'You seem to know an awful lot about what has been happening. I wonder what else you know.' He gestured in the direction of the cemetery gates. 'Shall we?'

'Can we not talk here?' She looked round at the sun dappling the trees and the grassed areas. 'It's so much more pleasant than one of your stuffy interview rooms.'

'As long as you repeat every word of it when we do go to Abbey Road.'

She nodded her assent.

'When you told my sergeant it was a dangerous world for children, I think you meant more than Emily's death. Cara left us a letter suggesting you can help with our inquiries.'

'She came to see me when my case against CG Haulage collapsed. Said Danny got drunk one night and admitted he was driving the truck that killed Emily. Said he had to tell someone, reckoned it had been preying on his mind.'

'I think he talked about a lot more than Emily's death, though. I think he was also talking about the sex ring.'

'You've read Cara's letter by now so you know the answer to that.'

'Why would she tell you all this? You weren't friends, I think?'

'I'd hardly ever met the woman, but she knew about the collapse of my legal action. Said she wanted me to know what kind of a man Danny was.'

'But why? Cara Galston did not strike me as the kind of woman to have a conscience.'

'I got the impression that Cara Galston only ever acts in her own self-interest.'

'So, what was her reason?'

'Does it matter? Surely what matters is that you can arrest them all now. Put an end to it.'

'How long had you known about the sex ring?'

'A few weeks.' Janice looked across the cemetery and shook her head. 'I was shocked when I heard. That such awful things could be going on under our noses for all those years defies belief. Those poor children.'

'I still cannot understand why Cara would tell a stranger. I mean, why choose you of all…' Blizzard's voice tailed off. 'Dear God, was Emily one of their victims?'

'No.' Janice shook her head vigorously and looked at the picture of her child beaming out of the gravestone. 'No, she was spared that, thank God. My Emily was a loved and treasured child who always felt safe.'

'But Jenny's kids did not, I think?'

'No, they didn't. Cara said that's why they were killed. Jenny started to suspect something was going on – I think Pauline told her – and she threatened to go the police. There's no way Danny could let that happen.'

'So, he killed them?'

'Danny Galston was a coward, Chief Inspector. All bullies are.'

'Are you saying he got someone else to do it?'

'I think we both know the answer to that.'

'Back to Lenny Rowles.'

'Back to Lenny Rowles. I think there may have been other murders as well.'

'Others?' asked Blizzard, feeling an icy chill running through his veins.

'Danny told Cara a couple of other kids were killed to keep their mouths shut.'

'Do you know their names?'

'I am sorry, all I know is that they were in care. A boy and a girl, Cara said. The girl was older. Cara said she thought they might have been brother and sister. Many wicked acts have been carried out in this city, Chief Inspector. Why did the police not do something about it?'

'You have no idea,' murmured Blizzard.

The chief inspector let his eyes wander momentarily and they settled on a man and his young daughter walking down one of the nearby paths, holding hands and chatting happily, the eight-year-old stopping to point excitedly at a squirrel scuttling up a tree. Janice followed the chief inspector's gaze and smiled.

'Not everyone is a victim,' she said, reading the chief inspector's thoughts. 'Some children are loved beyond words.'

'You know,' said Blizzard, recalling Colley's grin when he finally accepted that the arrival of the impending baby was an event to be celebrated, 'I think you are probably right, Mrs Garbutt.'

Chapter twenty-six

As darkness shrouded Hafton at six the next morning, the briefing room at Abbey Road Police Station was packed with officers, each one eagerly awaiting the arrival of John Blizzard. There was an electricity in the air and the assembled officers sat repeating half-heard snatches of conversation and speculating wildly. What everyone did know was that the impending operation was linked to the attacks on David Tulley and Alan Hayes. A strong sense of personal business to be finished was one of the reasons why so many had come in on days off. Everyone had heard that Lenny Rowles was back in the city. The officers knew that Rowles had, in his time, dispatched a number of their colleagues to the general hospital; one had even been forced to retire because of his injuries. The news that Lenny Rowles had returned meant that the waiting was over: this was payback time and no one was going to miss it.

Sitting amid the gathering, Fee Ellis tried hard to suppress her own excitement. Snatching an hour away from the frantic activity, the chief inspector had finally taken her into his confidence the afternoon before. As a woman whose thoughts had turned to the prospect of her own possible motherhood in recent months, she was reduced to tears more than once. Now, sitting in the briefing room, she glanced round and caught sight of Colley, who was in his usual position, leaning against the wall by the door. As Fee watched, he instinctively raised a hand to the bruise on his face. Catching her eye, Colley winked at Fee; she smiled back.

Standing next to the sergeant were two men she did not recognise but whom she surmised were Randall and Mather. Their presence in the room was attracting a lot of interest and a number of officers had already been over to shake their hands. Fee noted that most of them headed for Randall; Mather seemed more of a stranger to them and stood aloof, saying little and acknowledging the odd greeting with a slight smile as he waited quietly for the briefing to start.

Shortly after six, John Blizzard pushed his way through the door, followed by Arthur Ronald, and a hush fell on the room as the chief inspector surveyed each of them in turn. They could feel his eyes boring into them, a tactic he had used many times before in briefings, a deeply personal challenge to action. Ronald sat down at the side of the room, leaving the stage free for his friend; this was John Blizzard's show and few did it better.

'Ladies and gentlemen,' began Blizzard with the slightest of smiles. 'Thank you for turning up at such an unearthly hour and apologies to those nursing hangovers, especially those of you at Gary Mac's birthday party last night. Try not to throw up in the back of the paddy wagon, guys and gals.'

There were a few laughs and everyone glanced at several uniformed officers sitting in the corner of the room; they smiled ruefully and tried to ignore their throbbing heads.

'Talking of health,' said Blizzard, 'I imagine you would like to know the latest on the boys.'

Murmurs of agreement ran round the room.

'Hayesy is recovering nicely. As for Tulley...' Blizzard looked serious, evoking expressions of consternation from the assembled officers. 'I am afraid that after his initial good progress, he had to undergo surgery last night to extricate a corned beef pastie from his trouser pocket. Don't worry, though, the doctors say he's going to be OK and Tulley's going to have it for his breakfast.'

The comment was greeted with loud laughter – of relief more than at the joke – and Blizzard smiled then held up a hand, face suddenly solemn.

'I can now confirm what most of you will have heard anyway, namely that we believe that one of the men who carried out the attack to be Lenny Rowles. I imagine some of you have good reason to remember him.'

There were plenty of nodded heads and whispers ran round the room like the breeze through summer grass.

'So, to business,' said Blizzard, steel in his voice. 'This morning's operation is not just about Lenny Rowles. Many of you will have been aware of rumours over the years suggesting that there is a sex ring operating in this city. There have been those who dismissed the idea as fanciful – our own dear chief constable seems to have been somewhat sceptical – but many of you have not been so sure. I certainly have not, Arthur has not and, without going into detail, there are others in the room who have taken the same view.'

Colley allowed himself a smile; they had waited a long time for this moment.

'I can reveal that, thanks to work carried out by a number of officers over the past few days, we believe we are in a position to finally smash this ring apart. We believe that Lenny Rowles was part of the ring before he left the city. He and Danny Galston would appear to have been its enforcers, making sure no one dared speak to us. We believe that Danny Galston's death left the ring vulnerable. The leaders feared they were about to be exposed – we spoke last night to one of the editors of a Sunday tabloid and it seems Gerry Brauner was working on an investigation with a team of their reporters. The ring had worked out what was happening and brought Lenny Rowles back to sort it. Well, now it is us who are going to sort it.'

Excited whispering passed through the room again but Blizzard held up a hand. The room fell silent.

His voice was suddenly softer, 'Fifteen years ago, I stood in Danny Galston's house with Harry Roberts. We vowed that one day we would catch the man who murdered Jenny and the kids. Sadly, Harry never lived to see that day.'

All eyes were turned on the chief inspector.

'But I did.' Blizzard's voice was harsh, anger getting the better of him. 'The night Harry died, I promised him I would bring the killer to book. This morning, I will keep that promise, by God I will.'

The officers watched, fascinated by the strong emotions battling for supremacy within the chief inspector.

'And there is one more thing,' said Blizzard, regaining his calm. 'Myself and Harry made another promise, so please remember that we are also looking for Pauline Galston.'

He looked out of the window in the blackness of the rain-flecked morning before turning back to survey them.

'It's time to bring her home, ladies and gentlemen.'

Chapter twenty-seven

'Are you sure about this?' asked Colley.

'As sure as I can be,' said Blizzard, looking at his sergeant with eyes that gleamed in the half-light thrown by the street lamps.

They were sitting in Blizzard's car parked at end of a road not far from Abbey Road Police Station. The officers had initially stayed behind to watch the last of the police vehicles rumble out of the yard into the early morning darkness. With a satisfied grunt, Blizzard had then taken his car round to the front of the station, joined some moments later by Colley, the sergeant pulling on his black windcheater as he trotted briskly down the steps. They had driven slowly to their target house, neither speaking, each alone with their thoughts.

Many of the names on Cara Galston's list of ring members had surprised them but the top one more than most, and they had immediately realised the potential difficulties of confronting such people with only the flimsiest of evidence. They were also aware that Cara had fallen out with their target in recent days. Was she naming him in an act of calculated revenge? Everything else she had done had been well-planned, what about this? Was she somehow settling some old scores? Now, after a short drive through the mist, the detectives were sitting on a modern housing estate, its roads deserted and the detached houses in darkness as their occupants slumbered, unaware that they were being watched.

'She could be having us on,' commented Colley after a few moments.

'The thought had occurred. I would put nothing past the woman.'

Blizzard glanced in his rear-view mirror as another car pulled into the road behind them, cut its engine and extinguished its headlights.

'Randall.'

'Alex with him?'

'Yeah.'

'Guess he would not want to be miss out on this,' said Colley. He looked out at the houses with their carefully-coiffured lawns and creeping ivy winding its way elegantly across the mock-Elizabethan timbers. 'God, I hate all this.'

'Hate what?'

'This.' The sergeant gestured to their target's house. 'I mean, it's so plastic, guv. So... false. Take this fellow. His whole life has been a lie – assuming Cara is to be believed.'

'You seem unsure about that, though.'

'I guess you get this image of a paedophile.' Colley looked at the double garages and the lawns. 'And it's not this.'

'Perhaps that's the point. Perhaps that's how they avoid detection for so long. They've got a respectable façade and the money to pay people like Lenny Rowles to keep their victims quiet.'

'Maybe.'

'He *is* our man, David. I can almost taste it. Feels funny, though, being so close after all these years. I always wondered what it would feel like.'

'Not like this, I imagine.'

'I thought I would be sitting outside Danny Galston's house for a start.'

The car radio crackled into life.

'They're going in,' said Blizzard, listening to the sudden rush of messages over the airwaves.

The chief inspector instinctively turned to the sergeant and stretched out a hand. The sergeant shook it and gave a half-smile.

'Let's do this,' he said.

Blizzard nodded and the detectives got out of the car and walked towards the house. Behind them, Randall and Mather did likewise.

'Ready, gentlemen?' asked Blizzard, turning to face them as they gathered at the end of the drive.

'Too bloody right,' said Randall.

'I'll take the back,' said Mather, running up to the side gate and hurdling it in one smooth movement.

'I'll take the milk-float,' grinned Colley as a wheezing sound alerted them to the vehicle's arrival in the scene.

Blizzard and Randall chuckled as he ran out into the road and held up a hand to halt the float. After a hurried conversation with the driver, the sergeant returned and all three officers walked up to the front door. Blizzard's finger hovered over the bell for a moment.

'No time for doubts now,' said Randall, reaching past him and pressing.

The ringing seemed to reverberate around the silent estate and seconds later, lights went on upstairs and they heard feet on the stairs. The hall light went on and the security chain was unlocked, the door swinging open to reveal a startled-looking man in striped blue pyjamas. For a moment, he struggled to make out their features, silhouetted as they were in the glare of the security light, then his eyes widened as he recognised Blizzard.

'Brian Graham,' said the chief inspector. 'You are under arrest.'

* * *

By the time the officers returned to Abbey Road with their shaken and silent prisoner, the custody area was a hive of activity. Blizzard stood and watched, with grim satisfaction, a succession of men being brought in by his officers. Unshaven, wearing clothes hurriedly thrown on, they looked frightened and bewildered as they were processed and taken for questioning by teams of detectives. Unlike the scenes following the Regional Organised Crime Unit's arrests a few days before, there was no sense of triumph. The detectives all knew it was far too early to celebrate and were acutely aware that each man had strenuously denied being guilty of anything. That would be their tactic throughout the questioning, the officers suspected, and lawyers in sharp suits were already lining up to do battle. The chief inspector knew that the only evidence he had against their clients was a conversation with Janice Garbutt, a woman who had admitted attacking gravestones in an act of revenge, and a letter from Cara Galston, a woman whose motives were suspect to say the least.

Adding to the pressure on the chief inspector was the fact that the Keeper team had always known that, when it came to breaking apart the ring, they only had one shot at it. Get it wrong and the chance had gone for ever, the defences would become so watertight that the opportunity for further arrests would be lost. That is why Blizzard and Ronald had decided to move in now. Ordinarily, they would have taken more time to plan their approach but they both sensed that Cara Galston, for whatever reason, had opened a door that would soon be slammed shut again. Blizzard, ever the gambler, was revelling in the moment but, watching the prisoners gathering in the custody suite, he realised that the interviews about to start were crucial if four years of work were not to be wrecked.

The chief inspector turned to see Arthur Ronald walking towards him.

'My neck's on the bloody line with this one,' whispered Ronald in the chief inspector's ear. 'If Cara Galston is playing games, I'll be writing out parking tickets for the rest of my career.'

'What career?'

'I'm not kidding, John,' hissed Ronald. 'We've not just brought in a bunch of toe-rags here. Look at them, for God's sake. There's thirteen of them and they're all professional men. And that fellow over there, he runs one of the city's biggest aviation supply companies. What's more, I recognise at least half of them from the Rotary Club.'

'Jesus,' said Blizzard, turning to him with a look of mock-horror. 'Rotary? I did not realise that, Arthur. I'll have them all released immediately.'

'You know what I mean. These are respectable people. Pillars of the community. One of them even has a sodding MBE, for God's sake.'

'Yeah, but isn't that what we always guessed.'

'I know, I know, but if we're wrong, the chief will put my balls through the meat-grinder.'

'Bloody hell, there's the kind of image you don't want to think about too often.'

'Come on, I'm serious.'

'Relax, Arthur, we're right.' Blizzard gave a slight smile as he spied a familiar figure approaching. 'Hey up, here comes trouble.'

'Brilliant,' groaned Ronald.

Wendy Talbot walked purposefully across the room towards them.

'What's the bloody idea of this?' she snapped.

'And good morning to you, Wendy,' said Blizzard affably.

'Cut the smart-arse stuff! I've just heard that one of your teams has lifted Ralph Cargill.'

'Indeed, they have.' Blizzard glanced over as a couple of uniformed officers brought the haulage boss into the custody room. 'He seems remarkably dry for a man who's been swimming all this time.'

'Don't fuck about with me. We had an agreement, Blizzard. Ralph Cargill is mine.'

Was yours, Wendy.'

'What do you mean?'

'You may have gathered that we have broken up a major sex ring...'

'Actually, I hadn't,' she said irritably. 'None of your officers will tell me anything.'

'Doesn't feel very nice, does it?' said Ronald. 'So, as John says, we will be questioning him first. If you want to talk to Ralph Cargill about his truckload of pea-shooters, you'll have to do it later.'

'But we need him now. No one else is talking. Come on, guys, give me a break. I really need a breakthrough. There's a lot of shit flying.'

'All in good time,' said Blizzard. 'Hey, if you leave it with us, maybe we can solve your crime for you as well.'

Talbot glared at them, thought about saying something but instead stalked wordlessly across the room.

'Pea-shooters?' said Blizzard, looking at Ronald and raising an eyebrow.

'Well, what do you expect me to say?' said the superintendent, allowing himself a laugh as he watched Talbot brush roughly past Colley, who was carrying a couple of plastic cups of tea from the vending machine.

'I wish she'd stop doing that,' said the sergeant as he walked up to them and handed a cup to Blizzard before flicking away the drops of spilled tea from his jacket.

'So where did Cargill turn up?' asked Blizzard.

'Trying to get over the garden wall at Nick Jameson's house.'

'He's the architect, isn't he?'

'Yeah, and a worried one at that. I don't reckon he'll take much pushing.'

'Let's start pushing then,' said Blizzard.

Chapter twenty-eight

Blizzard and Colley were sitting in one of the interview rooms, surveying the 38-year-old architect with interest. When they had gone through the list supplied by Cara, some names had been familiar but there had been others which meant little to them. Jameson's was one and Colley's task the previous day had been to co-ordinate background research into them. That work had confirmed that Nick Jameson was a partner in an architects' firm operating out of the city centre and a man with a clean criminal record. Married but with no children, he was known as a respectable, clean-living man who was a valued member of the Rotary Club and the local quoits club.

A slim man with short brown hair and a complexion that was normally fresh-faced, he represented a very different picture now; unshaven with hair lank and uncombed, he was wearing a hurriedly thrown-on black T-shirt and jeans. And he had fear in his eyes. Jameson had been allowed a brief discussion with his lawyer and the solicitor had disappeared to make some phone calls. As the detectives waited for his return, they allowed the silence to lengthen and with each passing second, Jameson's agitation increased. After a few minutes, the door opened and in walked the lawyer, his demeanour still suggesting irritation at having been dragged out of bed by what he seemed to view as little more than a brief distraction.

'Can we get this nonsense over with as quickly as possible,' said the lawyer, sitting down.

'Certainly, Mr Pallister,' said Blizzard. He pointed to the pad and pen on the desk. 'If your client would like to jot down an admission of guilt, you can be on your way in plenty of time for breakfast.'

'My client will do no such thing. This whole thing is an absolute farce and I personally will see that heads roll. I happen to know your chief constable very well and I will be making a formal complaint, I can assure you.'

'Before you do, perhaps your client would like to explain why Ralph Cargill, a man sought by the police in connection with serious firearms-related offences, was found shinning over his garden wall an hour or so ago?'

'My client has no idea who this Mr Cargill is. He can only assume that the man had been hiding in his garden without his knowledge.'

'Perhaps he thought we wanted him for armed shrubbery.'

'I hardly think this is the time for humour, Chief Inspector,' snapped Pallister. 'Harbouring a fugitive is a very serious offence and my client strenuously denies such a preposterous suggestion.'

'According to an initial search of your client's property,' said Colley, glancing at his notes, 'someone had been staying in Mr Jameson's spare bedroom.'

'My client sometimes has friends round to stay. How can you be sure that the person in the room was Ralph Cargill?'

'Well, admittedly he did not have his name sown into his underpants,' said Colley.

'There you are then. It could have been anyone.'

'Not unless they had Ralph Cargill's wallet. He dropped it in his hurry to get out of the room.'

'Ok,' said Jameson guardedly, 'so Ralph was there.'

'Harbouring a felon is a serious offence,' said Blizzard.

Jameson nodded and they sensed a change in his demeanour, a sense of relief that he was not being questioned about the sex ring. He leaned over and whispered something to his lawyer.

'My client,' said Pallister eventually, 'wishes to make a statement. He realises that he has acted wrongly but this was an action bred of misguided loyalty to Mr Cargill, whom he has known for some years. He accepts that he has been naïve and would like to make a statement to that effect. He would also like to apologise for the trouble he has caused.'

Jameson nodded eagerly.

'Excellent,' said Blizzard.

'However, one thing has been troubling me,' continued the lawyer. 'I thought the investigation relating to Mr Cargill's haulage depot was being handled by the Regional Organised Crime Unit. Indeed, I fancy I saw DCI Talbot in the custody suite a little earlier. Should she not have been handling this interview, Chief Inspector?'

'It is amazing how many people have told me that she could do my job better than me. No, Mr Pallister, she should not be interviewing your client because Cargill's presence in your client's house is the least of his problems.'

The smug look that had pervaded Jameson's face as his lawyer made the statement suddenly faded and he looked anxiously at the detectives.

'You see,' said Blizzard, 'Ralph Cargill is also suspected of being a key part of a sex ring that has been operating in this city. We suspect Mr Jameson here is involved as well.'

The effect on Nick Jameson was startling. He gaped at the chief inspector then recoiled as if he had been struck across the face. Slumping back in his chair, he looked in horrified silence at Blizzard then the sergeant, his face ashen, eyes registering sheer terror. Even the lawyer looked surprised at the revelation and glanced with concern at his client. Blizzard allowed them to digest the information. He wanted to savour the moment, the moment he sensed that the breakthrough had finally come after so many fruitless years, years in which informants had offered tantalising snippets of information then clammed up when questioned further or simply disappeared into the shadows. Now, for the first time, Blizzard looked on a ring member who had found himself drawn out of those shadows and cruelly exposed. Blizzard felt his heart thumping. *Go on*, he said to himself fiercely, *go on*. None of this was apparent to Jameson or his lawyer, who looked upon the chief inspector's impassive features and wondered what more surprises the detective had in store for them.

'I do hope your client is not going to take ill,' said Blizzard. 'Throwing a wobbly does not tend to be a particularly helpful tactic when we have so many interesting things to talk about.'

'Oh, God,' moaned Jameson.

'I take it that our information is correct then?' said Blizzard.

The architect still looked as if he was about to collapse and the detectives surveyed him with increasing concern. It was not concern for Jameson's health, more anxiety that the interview would be disrupted and the moment gone for ever. They both knew that in such interviews, there came moments when all could be won and lost on the throw of a dice. This was one such moment, Blizzard had gambled but to their dismay, Nick Jameson rallied and, finding new strength, looked at the detectives with defiant eyes.

'I am saying nothing,' he said. 'These allegations are absolutely ridiculous.'

'I shall have to take advice from my client,' said Pallister, 'but I have to agree that they do sound preposterous. Mr Jameson...'

There was a knock on the interview room door and, making his excuses, chief inspector walked with heavy foot out into the corridor to be confronted by Alex Mather.

'This had better be good, Alex,' he said. 'Jameson has just clammed up and I suspect that was the deal among them all if they were ever lifted.'

'Well not everyone read the script then,' said Mather, who was as animated as Blizzard had ever seen him, his eyes bright, a nervous tension coursing through his body. 'I've been interviewing Edward Devereaux, you know the guy who runs that paper mill over on the east side. Turns out he left the ring two years ago.'

'And why would he do that?'

'Devereaux's daughter reached the age of five and he realised the ring was looking at her. Suddenly, he did not want to play anymore.'

'So, what has he said?'

'Reckons more than fifty kids have been abused down the years, and he confirmed the talk of murders. Reckons as many as six kids could have been murdered.'

'Jesus Christ!'

'When Galston was murdered, Devereaux decided the time was right to come and talk to us, ask for some kind of plea bargain. He was about to do that when...'

'Lenny Rowles came back?'

'Yeah, and that changed everything. Scared the shit out Devereaux so he kept quiet. But I reckon that as long as we keep him safe, he'll sing like a bird.'

Blizzard closed his eyes for a second; after all the years of waiting, he hardly dared believe it to be true. He opened his eyes again and placed a hand gently on Mather's shoulder.

'Good work, matey-boy,' he said. 'Bloody good work.'

Mather grinned; it struck Blizzard that he had never seen him do that in all the years he had known him.

'Did he mention Nick Jameson by any chance?' asked Blizzard. 'I'd love to wipe the smile off that lawyer's face.'

'Yes, he did. Devereaux reckons Jameson felt the same doubts. His little girl is growing up and he was just as frightened that they would start on her. She's called Amy, if you want to use that in the interview. Quite a few of the victims were their own kids.'

'Jesus,' murmured Blizzard quietly. 'What the hell have we unearthed, Alex?'

The chief inspector went back into the interview room, trying to control the strong emotions crowding into his mind.

'Well, well, Mr Jameson,' said Blizzard as he sat down, 'it seems one of your little friends has dropped you in it.'

'I have already said that I am innocent of these prep...'

'Tell me about Amy. Was she next?'

'I don't know what you mean,' said Jameson.

'Come on, Nick, we know you were thinking about coming to us,' said Blizzard, pushing a pencil and pad across the table. 'Get writing. For Amy's sake, because if we let your mates free, they are sure as hell coming for her. Is that what you want?'

Jameson stared at him then suddenly seemed to cave in. He sat in silence for a few moments, his body wracked with huge sobs. Blizzard sat back and let him weep. Jameson was broken and everyone in the room knew it.

* * *

Half an hour later, having left Colley with Jameson still penning his statement, the chief inspector walked down the corridor to the CID room with a light step and was surrounded by excited officers, all wanting to update him on their inquiries. The news was encouraging; although many of the arrested men were refusing to talk, one or two were showing signs of wishing to unburden themselves in return for a more lenient sentence as they realised that the conspiracy was crumbling around them. Blizzard answered the queries from his officers as best he could and walked purposefully towards the interview room containing Ralph Cargill.

Blizzard found a frustrated Max Randall sitting at the desk opposite Cargill. Next to the haulier sat his lawyer, a shaven-headed young man in a grey designer suit. Blizzard scowled; he hated lawyers and he hated designer clothes. He also hated Philip Gorton. The chief inspector's last encounter with the solicitor was the previous year, during an inquiry into a local businessman alleged to have been laundering money for a local drugs gang. Blizzard had fought the Regional Organised Crime Unit for the right to handle the case and had been acutely embarrassed when the smooth-talking Gorton managed to get all charges dropped. Gorton gave a slight smile as Blizzard sat down.

During the hour of questioning that followed, Cargill did not say much either, retaining his composure and parrying everything with a non-committal answer while his lawyer constantly interrupted to challenge the detectives on points of law. Blizzard could see that Max Randall was getting irritated by the tactic.

'Listen, Ralph,' Randall growled eventually, 'this is getting us nowhere and your lawyer should be advising you to co-operate.'

'I am co-operating. You have got the wrong man.'

'My client is right,' said the lawyer. 'From the questions you have been asking, you appear to be fishing rather. I have not seen any indication that you have even the smallest shred of evidence.'

'I think we have a little more than that,' said Blizzard.

'Come on, Chief Inspector. We can guess where this information has come from. Any decent defence barrister would tear Cara Galston to shreds. Do you really think she can be trusted?'

'She was most specific about your client.'

'Of course she was, but I am most surprised that you cannot see her little game. For years, she tried to persuade

Danny to attempt to buy my client out of the company. When Danny died, Cara saw her chance.'

'Yeah,' said Cargill. 'With me in prison, she can mount a strong case to buy the company outright. Brian Graham reckons she already has a buyer lined up.'

'She also named Brian Graham as involved in the sex ring.'

'And do you want to know why?' said Cargill. 'Because Brian thought better of helping her so she sacked him. She's a vindictive little bitch.'

'So, you see,' said the lawyer, clipping shut his briefcase, 'unless you have anything more than the ramblings of a spiteful woman, I suggest we end this interview and you let my client go about his lawful business.'

'A nice try,' said the chief inspector. 'However, it would be remiss of me to let your client go without giving our colleagues on the Regional Organised Crime Unit the opportunity to talk to you about the guns found at his depot.'

'I think you will find,' said Gorton, standing up, 'that we can answer all their questions about that unfortunate misunderstanding as well.'

'Just stay there,' snapped Blizzard. 'We have not finished yet.'

The chief inspector glanced at Randall; both men knew they had.

* * *

Graham Ross stood in the gloom of the GC Haulage garage, his nostrils filled with the smell of oil and dirt. His forensics team had been searching the depot for an hour but had found nothing to link the company with the activities of a sex ring. Ross glanced around him: in a corner of the dimly-lit garage, one of his team was meticulously taking fingerprints from tool cabinets and in another, two more were grunting as they strained to move rusty old pipes that looked like they had been lain across the floor for years. Ross closed his eyes and heard again the words of John Blizzard. *Let the scene talk to you. Listen to its words.*

'Easy for you to say,' sighed Ross, opening his eyes.

'I reckon we're wasting our time here,' said one of his officers, cursing as one of the pipes slipped out of his hands.

Ross tensed. Something about the sound of the pipe on the floor had alerted his attention. The others had heard it, too. Ross stepped forward and stamped his boot on the floor where the pipe had been. It made a different muffled sound, a hint of hollowness beneath. Ross knelt down and reached out a hand to run it slowly through the dust on the floor, his fingers probing carefully.

'I'm not sure the concrete is as thick as the rest,' he said at length.

'There,' said one of the forensics officers, pointing to a faint crack.

'Jesus,' breathed Ross, 'that's a trapdoor.'

After a few minutes exertion, they managed to prize open the door, which revealed itself as a piece of wood lined with a thin layer of concrete to avoid detection. One of the officers flashed a torch down the hatch, from which was emanating an unpleasant musty smell. For a few moments, they knelt and surveyed in silence the child's sleeping bag folded up in one corner of the fetid little space.

* * *

Back in the interview room, after another thirty minutes of fruitless questioning of Cargill by the detectives, Philip Gorton took hold of his briefcase once more and stood up.

'Accept it, Chief Inspector,' he said. 'You are wasting your time.'

Blizzard sighed and was about to nod his assent when there was a knock on the door. With the solicitor sitting back down, Blizzard walked out into the corridor to a beaming Graham Ross.

'It had better be good,' said Blizzard darkly.

'You are just going to love me.'

Five minutes later, after a conversation in which the chief inspector became more and more animated, Blizzard took a moment or two to calm himself down, restored his deadpan expression and walked back into the interview room. He gave Cargill a knowing smile; sensing that something had changed, the haulier returned the look uneasily.

'That was my forensics officer,' said Blizzard. 'His team has been searching your client's depot…'

'I think you will find that the Regional Organised Crime Unit did that after the raid,' said Gorton, a hint of mockery in his voice. 'They found nothing, so I can't really see…'

'I am not sure their search was particularly thorough. After all, they had the guns and that was all they were looking for. No, my team was looking for something else, a sign that children had been taken to the depot.'

The smile was wiped from Cargill's face and he looked at his lawyer for support. Gorton said nothing, unnerved by the new-found assurance in Blizzard's voice.

'And guess what?' continued the chief inspector. 'It looks like your client has been having sleepovers, Mr Gorton.'

'Jesus Christ,' breathed Cargill, glancing around him as if seeking some kind of escape.

'Now you know how those kids felt,' said Blizzard, his voice suddenly fierce. 'You are trapped and by the time we have finished, I am going to nail you and your little bunch of scumbags to the fucking wall. And, yes, Mr Gorton, you can use that in any complaint you may wish to submit to my chief constable.'

The lawyer opened his mouth to remonstrate but something in Blizzard's expression suggested it would be a bad idea.

Chapter twenty-nine

Blizzard left Randall and walked to one of the other interview rooms. Joined by Colley on the way, he entered the room to find Brian Graham sitting nervously at the table. He was dressed in grubby white shirt and trousers thrown on when he was arrested and, although he was trying to look calm, the fear showed behind his eyes. His solicitor, a thin, balding man in a pale grey suit sat next to him.

'I would like an explanation as to why my client has been kept waiting so long,' he said.

'Yes, I am sorry about that,' said Blizzard, giving the solicitor a disarming smile. 'We have a lot to do, as I am sure you can appreciate.'

'Yes, and I want to know what is going on, Chief Inspector.'

'Your client was arrested on suspicion of involvement with the murders of the Galston family 15 years ago.'

'Preposterous!' exclaimed Graham, springing to his feet.

'Actually, I think it probably is, Mr Graham.'

'You do?' said the accountant, sitting down again.

His lawyer looked equally taken aback. Colley said nothing; his body language did the speaking for him as he sat back with arms folded and pursed lips, refusing to look at the chief inspector.

'Yes,' said Blizzard. 'You see, Mr Graham, we acted in good faith when we brought you in. You had been named as the leader of a child sex ring which has been responsible for a number of murders, including the Galston girls.'

'Named by whom?' demanded Graham.

'Cara Galston.'

'Are you really going to take the word of a woman like her over someone like me?'

'We now realise that she probably named you out of spite because you refused to handle the purchase of CG Haulage for her. In fact, Mr Graham, you have shown yourself to be a man of great moral standing and I apologise for the way you have been treated. You are a victim in all of this.'

'Be that as it may,' blurted out Colley, unable to contain himself any longer, 'she did name him, guv. She seems to have been right about all the others, why not about him?'

'I think we should discuss this later,' said Blizzard.

'But…'

'Leave it,' snapped Blizzard, looking sharply at the sergeant.

Colley looked as if he was about to challenge the statement then shrugged and sat back, folding his arms once more and eying the chief inspector furiously.

'Perhaps,' said the lawyer, standing up and giving Colley a smug look, 'you should learn to be less impetuous, Sergeant. I take it my client is free to go now, Chief Inspector?'

Colley bit his lip but said nothing as Blizzard wafted a hand wearily at the door.

'I will be submitting a formal complaint about this,' said the lawyer tartly as he led his client out into the corridor.

'I am sure you will,' said Blizzard. 'The others are putting theirs on a pile by the front door, you might want to do the same.'

When a uniformed constable had led Graham and his lawyer out into the corridor, the chief inspector turned to Colley.

'And as for you,' said Blizzard. 'You have shown yourself capable of sinking to the very depths of deceit.'

'I like to oblige,' said the sergeant. 'But are you sure this will work? If we lose him, that's worse that Wendy Talbot letting Ralph Cargill slip through her fingers. We'll never hear the last of it.'

'You do sound like Arthur sometimes. And, no, I am not sure it will work. Who have you got tailing him?'

'Fee and Bobby B are on first turn.'

'That's another night making my own sodding dinner,' said Blizzard. He smiled as Mather walked in with a pleased expression on his face. 'And what's tickled your fancy, young man?'

'It's all unravelling, guv,' said Mather, sitting down in the seat recently vacated by Brian Graham. 'They're all trying to save their skins now. All they want to do is cut deals.'

'Anyone say anything about Barry Lawson?' asked Colley, thinking back to his informant's body on the mortuary slab.

'Seems he procured a lot of the kids when he worked in social services. Went into a lot of care homes, apparently.'

'God, did I misjudge him,' said Colley.

'Hindsight is a wonderful thing,' said Blizzard. 'So, who killed Lawson? Lenny Rowles?'

'Looks like it. Seems they knew he was talking to Dave. There's someone else keeps being mentioned. That photographer bloke Gerry Brauner. The gang suspected he was trying to break the story and Graham became paranoid, kept ringing him and telling him to keep his trap shut. When they brought Lenny Rowles back, he decided that Brauner and Cara had to go. Looks like they got away, though.'

'There's time enough for them,' said Blizzard. 'Time enough.'

Chapter thirty

All was quiet in Hafton Cemetery at 5am the next morning, the stones silent sentinels to the finale of yet another human drama. Blizzard and his dozen-strong team had arrived half an hour previously, alerted by a call from the surveillance shift that had been parked outside Brian Graham's house for much of the night, taking over from Fee and her partner shortly after nine. At first, it seemed that they had been wasting their time because the accountant had stayed indoors for most of the time.

However, shortly after four, he left the house and drove to one of the city's council estates, arriving at the door of a maisonette to pick up a man whose bulky, silhouetted figure the watching officers recognised as it picked its way across the walkway and down onto the weed-infested quadrangle. The surveillance team felt a thrill of excitement as they crouched among the trees, watching Rowles digging up the grave of Susan Graham, her husband shooting furtive glances around, each one sending the watching officers crouching lower.

'Relax,' growled Rowles, looking up at him and leering. 'They can't hurt you, they're all dead.'

'Show more bloody respect, for God's sake! One of them happens to be my wife.'

'Yeah, and some respect you showed her,' said Rowles, returning to his digging.

Graham looked away. The watching officers could see the uneasy expression on his face. Blizzard and the team watched as Rowles dug, impervious to their presence, while Graham paced around nervously, occasionally glancing at his watch and sometimes peering into the darkness around them. Eventually, there was the sound of spade hitting timber and, with some difficulty, the two men hauled up the coffin. Rowles produced a crowbar and levered open the lid.

'The last place we would ever look,' murmured Colley.

'Let's do this,' said Blizzard.

He walked forward and flashed a torch at the two men. Graham cried out and tried to run but Mather hurled himself from behind a tree and knocked him to the ground, where the accountant lay winded. Rowles gave an enraged roar, snatched up the spade and swung it at the onrushing Colley. The sergeant ducked and Rowles sprinted away through the trees, still clutching the tool. Two shadowy figures emerged in front of him, half-illuminated by the flashing torchlight, but Rowles veered round them and continued to run in the direction of the entrance, showing remarkable pace for a big man. Colley sprinted after him, hurdling graves, his feet thundering on the soft earth as he closed on the fleeing Rowles. As Rowles reached the front gate, he realised that the sergeant was still behind him and whirled round, glowering at his pursuer. For a moment or two he backed up until he bumped against the gates then looked wildly about him for a way out. Finding nothing, he returned his gaze to the sergeant.

'Nowhere to run, Lenny,' said the sergeant.

'I should have finished you off at the playing field.'

'Come on, give it up,' said the sergeant.

'Never,' said Rowles and lunged forward.

Colley was too slow to react and the spade caught him full in the face, the sergeant hollering in pain and staggering backwards. As Colley sprawled on the ground, Rowles took a step forward and raised the spade to administer the final blow.

'Not a good idea, Lenny,' said a voice and Rowles looked up to see John Blizzard walking towards him.

'You!'

'Yeah, me, Lenny-boy. Been waiting a long time for this. There's a lot of people want to talk to you.'

Looking beyond the chief inspector, Rowles could see other officers approaching and noticed that two of them were pointing firearms at him. He looked back at Blizzard, seemingly uncertain as to his next move.

'See,' said Blizzard, 'it really is over, Lenny.'

'One more step!' snarled the killer, holding the spade high above his head and looking down at the prostrate Colley. 'One more step and your pal gets it.'

'I don't think so,' said Blizzard. 'See, if you move so much as a muscle, the firearms officers will drop you where you stand.'

'Maybe that would be for the best,' said Rowles, the fire in his eyes dimmed for a second. 'I ain't going back to prison.'

'I assume it was you who killed Jenny and the kids?' said Blizzard.

'I ain't saying nothing.'

'You don't need to,' said Blizzard, keeping an eye on the spade still held above Rowles' head. 'Let me tell you what I think happened. I reckon you were supposed to murder Jenny to shut her up and frighten the kids into keeping quiet. But I reckon it got out of hand – Jenny fought back, Chloe started to scream and Pauline escaped. In the end, you had no option, but I do not think Danny Galston ever wanted them dead.'

'Not sure he ever cared that much about them,' said Rowles, lowering the spade slightly. 'He was abusing them, what kind of a father does that make him?'

'It's a good question, Lenny.'

'Anyhow, you can't prove anything, Blizzard. It's all guesswork.'

'Oh, but I think we can. There's enough people prepared to point the finger at you now. And we've got you for Barry Lawson's murder anyway. So, let the sergeant go and we can discuss how this plays out.'

Rowles considered the comment then lowered the spade and gave a nod. The sergeant scrambled out of the way and joined Blizzard. Rowles looked at them and nodded.

'Wise choice,' said Blizzard.

Rowles threw away the spade and dived into a nearby bush before anyone could react, then he crashed through bushes and careered past gravestones in his desperate attempt to reach the main road. Colley and other officers gave chase and the firearms team started running, too. Rowles reached the perimeter hedge a fraction of a second before Colley, turned and gave an enraged bellow and snapped out a fist. Colley jerked backwards, lifted off his feet by the power of the blow, smashing his head against a gravestone as he fell. Rowles took a step forward and aimed a vicious kick at the sergeant's head. Colley's last image before he lost consciousness was the big man suddenly stiffening, his face a mask of disbelief as a single retort cut through the stillness of the night. After that, all went black for the sergeant.

* * *

When Colley regained consciousness several minutes later, he found himself lying in the grass near the gates, acutely conscious of the smell of damp earth. Opening his eyes, he groaned at the pain from his head then saw Blizzard walking towards him.

'Rowles?' asked the sergeant, attempting to sit up.

Blizzard nodded to the big man's body lying a few metres away, blood seeping from the bullet wound in the centre of his forehead.

'Had to be,' said Colley quietly. He tried to get to his feet.

'Hey, hey,' said the chief inspector, gently pushing him back as the sergeant's world began to swirl. 'Take it easy, you have taken a nasty knock to the head.'

Colley lay back down, closing his eyes. After a few seconds, he opened them again: Blizzard was still there.

'Brian Graham?' asked the sergeant.

'Gave up without a fight. Once a coward, always a coward.'

'And Pauline? Did you find her body?'

Blizzard nodded sadly and Colley closed his eyes again. The chief inspector turned and stared into the darkness, half expecting to see the strange little girl but there was no one there. The chief inspector knew in that moment that she would never come back. Perhaps his doctor had been right: perhaps it wasn't about her ghost at all, perhaps it had always been about his own. Now both could be laid to rest. Suddenly, the chief inspector's back gave a twinge and Blizzard smiled: in a funny way, it was a reassuring sensation.

* * *

'I can't go,' said Georgia Horwood.

It was shortly after nine that morning and Cara Galston and Gerry Brauner were standing in the departure lounge of Manchester Airport. The three of them had spent several days living as fugitives, moving from guest house to guest house, skulking in the shadows lest either Lenny Rowles or the police come looking for them. After the attack in Cara's house, they had taken a taxi to pick up Georgia but abandoned their initial plan to fly out the next morning because Gerry Brauner required hospital treatment for his injuries. Deciding not to seek it in Hafton, where too many people knew him and where the police would be looking for them, they travelled to Manchester and now that Brauner was fit enough to travel, they had arrived at the airport, which was when Georgia dropped her bombshell.

'What do you mean you can't go?' asked Cara.

'I have to go back to Hafton.'

'Why?' asked Brauner, dark glasses hiding his bruised eyes.

'You know why.'

'But you'll be safe once we get out of the country.'

'My mind is made up,' said Georgia. 'We started this together and we must end it together. I'm sorry.'

She turned and walked quickly from the airport. The flight was called and Cara Galston and Gerry Brauner were on their way.

Chapter thirty-one

Brian Graham sat silently in the interview room, staring anxiously at Blizzard and Max Randall. Graham's solicitor sat beside him. It was shortly after 11am and they had been waiting there some time for the detectives to arrive. When they did, the lawyer could contain his irritation no longer.

'Yet again, you have acted in an underhand manner, Chief Inspector,' he said. 'My client was tricked.'

'Sometimes the means justifies the end, Mr Ratcliffe. Your client has lied consistently to us and we needed to find a way of getting some semblance of truth out of him.'

'You have nothing on him, Chief Inspector. Nothing at all and the way you have gone about this will be the subject of an official…'

'Let me tell you how this will pan out. A number of your client's associates in the sex ring have named him as its leader. Their evidence alone will be enough to send him away for a very long time.'

'It's their word against mine!' exclaimed Graham.

'Then there is the little matter of discovering you digging up Pauline's Galston's body from your wife's grave.'

'I knew nothing about that! I was as shocked as you were when we found her.'

'So how do you explain your presence there?'

'Lenny Rowles made me do it.'

'I think not. Sergeant, enlighten our Mr Graham, please.'

Graham looked anxiously at Randall.

'Early today,' said the sergeant, 'forensics officers went to a rented factory unit on Wainscott Lane. It appears to be in your name, Mr Graham.'

The accountant's face drained of colour.

'Planning to manufacture widgets, were you?' asked Blizzard.

Graham gaped at him, unable to speak.

'Our examination is in its early stages,' continued Randall, 'but there is already enough to link it to the abuse of children.'

'I know nothing about that. Nothing at all.'

'Oh, for fuck's sake!' exclaimed Blizzard. He banged a fist on the table, startling the others. 'I am sick of your lies. Start telling us the sodding truth.'

Graham stared at him, fear in his eyes. The lawyer said nothing, taken aback by the flash of anger, exactly the reaction Blizzard was seeking. The advantage had swung his way and the time had come to ram it home.

'Besides, that is not all,' said the chief inspector, calming down. 'Several of the people we arrested yesterday said you ordered Rowles to attack Jenny Galston and the kids. I think something spooked Rowles and he had to flee the house with Pauline. But he couldn't let her live because she could identify him. Then when you realised we were getting close, you decided to move the body.'

'You cannot prove that,' blurted out Graham.

'Oh, but I think we can.'

'No,' said Graham desperately. 'All this was Lenny's idea. OK, I admit it, I knew he killed Jenny and the kids but it was nothing to do with me, honest to God.'

'But you do admit to being part of the sex ring?' said Randall.

Graham hesitated then glanced at his lawyer, who shrugged, Graham nodded.

'So we are finally getting somewhere,' said Blizzard. He sat back in satisfaction. 'And you are telling me it was all Rowles' fault?'

'Everything,' said Graham eagerly. 'I hated what was happening and got out.'

'When?'

'After Jenny and the kids died. It sickened me,' said Graham, his voice little more than a whisper. 'I realised the wicked things I had done and got out. Honest to God, that is what happened.'

'And did the ring continue after you left?' asked Randall.

'How would I know? I had no more involvement after that and I am as shocked as you are to find that my rented factory was being used for such purposes. Look, I will co-operate entirely with your inquiry. I'll tell you about how Danny offered up his kids. I'll tell you how Ralph Cargill was involved. I'll tell you everything. However, I would like to think that we could come to some kind of deal to protect my interests.'

Blizzard looked at him intently, trying to restrain the triumph he was feeling, not at Graham's admissions, which he knew had been cynically offered to save himself, but at the moment about to come. Randall glanced over at the chief inspector. His expression was impassive but it spoke volumes.

'Well,' said Blizzard. 'It has taken a lot of time but finally you are beginning to tell us the truth, Brian.'

'I admit I was wrong to mislead you,' said Graham, his confidence growing.

'I take it you had no idea Rowles was coming back?'

'No, I was shocked when I heard. Someone must have rung him.'

'Indeed they must. Any idea who?'

'Someone from within the ring, I imagine.'

Blizzard nodded at Randall and the sergeant produced a document from his pocket.

'Do you know what this is?' asked Randall.

Graham shook his head.

'These are the phone records from your office. Seems that the day Danny Galston was murdered, you made several calls to a number in Spain.'

'I have a friend there.'

'Indeed you have,' said Randall. 'The numbers were traced to a flat in Fuengirola. It belongs to a security guard at one of the clubs over there. We faxed a picture of Lenny Rowles to the police out there, taken from his days in Hafton, and guess what?'

Graham went white.

'Yes, you've guessed it,' said Randall. 'They appear to be one and the same man. Then lo and behold, what happens? Lenny comes back to Hafton and all hell breaks loose.'

Graham glanced at his lawyer for help.

'I really do think I need time with my client,' said Ratcliffe.

'From what I can see,' said Blizzard, 'he is going to have plenty of that.'

* * *

That afternoon Blizzard and Colley, the latter with a plaster over his gashed face, stood at the entrance to Hafton Cemetery. Neither spoke as two figures made their way along the main path towards the gates. As they arrived, Blizzard stepped forward. Georgia Horwood and Janice Garbutt looked at him with an expression of resignation. An hour later, they were all sitting in one of the interview rooms at Abbey Road Police Station, the women looking pale yet calm.

Blizzard leaned forward.

'Which of you delivered the fatal blow on Danny?' he asked.

'We did it together,' said Georgia. 'It seemed the best way.'

Janice Garbutt nodded.

'Either of you want to tell us why you killed him?'

'They say revenge is a dish best served cold, Chief Inspector,' said Janice. 'Well, I had been waiting for a long, long time.'

'I assume the collapse of the legal action was the catalyst?'

'My last chance of justice for my daughter had gone. I had nothing to live for.'

'And you?' asked Blizzard, turning to Georgia.

'It seemed the only thing to do. I went to see Janice, we talked about it and decided that he had to die.'

'But why not come to us?' asked Blizzard.

'Tell me, Chief Inspector,' said Georgia softly, 'when you went into that house fifteen years ago and saw little Chloe's body, what did you feel?'

Blizzard was transported once more back to the scene and experienced once more the salty taste of tears at the back of his throat.

'I felt rage,' he said. 'They didn't deserve that.'

'No child does,' said Colley.

'So, you look me in the face now and tell me that you do not understand what I did.'

Colley shook his head.

'I can't,' he said. 'I can't.'

Chapter thirty-two

'So, what's all this malarkey about going to live abroad?' asked Blizzard, reaching for his glass of wine.

Colley shrugged. 'It was just an idea,' he said.

'So, explain it.'

It was shortly before eleven the following Saturday evening and the officers, as well as Jay and Fee, were sitting in the living room of the terraced house which Colley shared with his girlfriend. Feeling dog-tired after the week's events, Blizzard had considered crying off but it was Jay's birthday and Fee persuaded him that a night out with friends might relax him a little. After enjoying their meal, they retired to the living room where they now sat amid pastel shades and soft light afforded by a couple of table lamps and the warmth of a flickering fake coal fire. Mellow music was playing quietly in the background and Blizzard was lounging in an armchair with a glass of wine in hand. The sergeant was in another chair, nursing a pint of beer and the girls were sitting on the sofa, sipping brandies. They all waited for Colley to answer the question.

'So,' repeated Blizzard. 'Explain it. Why on earth do you want to go and live abroad?'

'I don't know. I just quite fancy it, you know, away from this place.'

'I love Italy but there is no way I want to live there,' said Blizzard. 'It's OK on a holiday but you try getting a washer changed on your taps.'

'Yes, I know all that but...' began Colley. His voice tailed off.

'What he should really be saying,' said Jay, 'is that he does not want to bring a child up in this country. That's what he really thinks.'

Colley looked uncomfortable that the subject had come up. Something that had increasingly occupied his mind for a number of months, the sergeant nevertheless still found it difficult to air openly and the events of the week had only served to heighten the tensions within him. Time and time again he had found himself wondering if he had revealed too much when he and Blizzard had their conversation in the engine shed a few nights before. It was not the kind of thing men talked about, surely? Clearly, John Blizzard did.

'And what is your take on this?' asked the chief inspector, eying Jay keenly.

'It sounds brilliant, sitting in a little bar looking out over the Med with a glass of red in your hand, but when you get back home, not so simple.'

'But do you not see where I am coming from?' asked Colley, looking at his boss.

'I know the grass is always greener.'

'But bringing a child into the world is a big responsibility,' said Colley. 'You have to do what's best for them and it's not just child abuse. I mean, drugs are everywhere and every time we lift a dealer there's another one to take his place. And when they do get to court, some magistrate with a nice hat and no idea about real life gives them a gentle slap on the wrist. Even the judges are too soft. Now, if I were in charge of...' His voice tailed off as he noticed their amused looks.

'What?' he asked.

No one replied but their smiles grew broader.

'Was I ranting?' he asked ruefully.

'You'd slipped into Blizzard-speak,' said Fee. 'If we'd let you go any longer, you'd have been advocating hanging for anyone who drops litter.'

'Bloody good idea,' said Blizzard. 'I might suggest that next time I meet the chief constable.'

'Sorry,' said Colley with a wry smile, 'but I have been thinking a lot about this and I do wonder what kind of a world we will bring our child into.'

'One,' said Jay, reaching out to take his hand, 'where most of our kids are perfectly decent young people trying to make their way in life, just like they always did and always will. And the reason they feel as safe and secure as they do that is because of people like us. Parents. Teachers. Cops. That's why you can't go and run your bar just yet, David. You've got work to do here.'

'Do you know,' said Blizzard, 'you are going to make one hell of a mother.'

Epilogue

It was a pleasant early summer afternoon and John Blizzard stood in Hafton Cemetery, enjoying the warmth of the sun on his back and the sound of the birds. Since the events of six months previously, he had found himself visiting the cemetery less and less, but this time something had drawn him back. That morning, the last of the sex ring members had been jailed, Brian Graham had been given a life sentence for conspiracy to murder Jenny Galston and her children. The Keeper team had been there, Colley breaking his paternity leave, and celebrated with a drink in a quiet pub near the court afterwards. It was a strange atmosphere, as if they sensed that they would never sit together in the same room again, and when they left, the embraces were strong and heartfelt. In the previous weeks, eleven other ring members had been jailed. As for Georgia Horwood and Janice Garbutt, they admitted murdering Danny Galston and were given life sentences.

And now it was all over.

Blizzard felt weary as he walked over the gravestone and looked down at the inscription.

Jenny Galston

Born July 9, 1973
Died November 13, 2002
Aged 29

Chloe Galston
Born April 4, 1995
Died November 13, 2002
Aged 7

And her beloved sister
Pauline Galston
Born June 24, 1992
Died November 13, 2002
Aged 10

Together for eternity. Rest in peace in the arms of the Lord.

'Together again,' murmured Blizzard. He looked up to the sky. 'Got them, Harry boy. Got them all for you.'

He turned and saw Colley walking towards him with a pushchair.

'Thought I would see you here,' said the sergeant.

'First time out on your own with the little 'un?' asked Blizzard, looking down at the sleeping baby.

'Yeah,' said Colley. 'Jay's knackered so I thought I'd take the plunge.'

'Good for you,' said Blizzard, crouching down and gently touching the baby's ruddy cheek. 'And how is little Laura?'

'She's bloody brilliant,' said the sergeant. He looked at his friend, a troubled expression on his face. 'Can I ask you something?'

'As long as it isn't about nappies.'

'No, it's not.'

'Go on.'

'You know you always wondered if someone was protecting the sex ring, someone inside the force? Do you still think that?'

'Why do you ask?'

'I've been thinking – you do a lot of thinking when you're up in the middle of the night with a baby – Harry Roberts, when he said he hoped the Galston family could forgive him...'

The sergeant took a step back at the chief inspector's expression.

'Sorry,' he said, holding up his hands. 'Out of order.'

'It's not out of order, David, but I don't think he was protecting anyone. I think Harry felt guilty that he failed to catch Lenny Rowles, simple as that. On the question of bent coppers, Wendy Talbot reckons her mole was some girl in the typing pool.'

'Good.' He paused. 'There's something else. A personal matter.'

'Go on.'

'Well, it's a bit embarrassing but me and Jay have been talking, and we wondered if you would be Laura's godfather?'

'But I don't believe in God and I detest children.'

'Exactly. We can't think of anyone better qualified.' The sergeant looked at Blizzard anxiously. 'Will you do it?'

Blizzard turned away so that Colley could not see the huge grin on his face.

'I guess I just might,' he said.

THE END

List of Characters

Hafton Police:

DCI John Blizzard – head of Western Division CID
DS David Colley
DS Max Randall
DI Graham Ross – head of forensics in Western Division
DC Fee Ellis
DC David Tulley
DC Alan Hayes
DC Alex Mather

County force:

Det Supt Arthur Ronald – head of CID in the southern half of the force
Det Supt Wendy Talbot – head of the Regional Organised Crime Unit

Others:

Gerry Brauner – freelance photographer
Danny Galston – haulage company owner

Cara Galston – Danny's wife
Ralph Cargill – haulage company owner
Janice Garbutt – acquaintance of Cara Galston
Brian Graham – an accountant
Georgia Horwood – friend of Cara Galston
Nick Jameson – an architect
Barry Lawson – police informant
Jay Priest – Colley's partner
Peter Reynolds – Home Office Pathologist
Desmond Roach – cemetery manager
Lenny Rowles – Hafton criminal

If you enjoyed this book, please let others know by leaving a quick review on Amazon. Also, if you spot anything untoward in the paperback, get in touch. We strive for the best quality and appreciate reader feedback.

editor@thebookfolks.com

www.thebookfolks.com

ALSO BY JOHN DEAN

The next two books in this series

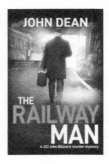

Veteran crime-solver DCI John Blizzard is confronted with his hardest case yet when a boxer and wide boy is found dead in a railway signal box. Someone is determined to ruin the investigation and prepared to draw the residents of a local housing estate into a war with the police to get their way. Has the detective finally met his match?

While detective John Blizzard looks into a series of drug-related deaths, his nemesis, gangland thug Morrie Raynor, is released from prison. Blizzard becomes convinced Raynor is linked to a new crime spree, but with little evidence other than the ravings of a sick, delirious man, the detective's colleagues suspect his personal feelings are clouding his judgement.

The DCI Jack Harris series

Detective Chief Inspector Jack Harris is a former soldier who, as a youth, fled his life in a remote North Pennines valley when he began to get involved in crime. Having joined the Army and then worked as a police officer in Manchester, the northern hills drew him back, as he always knew they would.

A man who would rather devote his time to walking the dogs, he finds instead that his job running CID requires him to deal with the effects of isolation on the community and the impact of criminals who travel in from outside the area to commit offences.

Begin this classic British detective mystery series with
DEAD HILL.

All FREE with Kindle Unlimited and available in paperback!

Other titles of interest

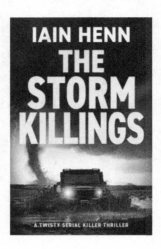

THE STORM KILLINGS by Iain Henn

As tornado season gets under way, the FBI's advanced computer system highlights an anomaly in the casualties. It looks like someone is using the chaos caused by the weather as cover to kill unsuspecting women in their homes. Special Agent Ilona Farris heads into the eye of the storm to catch them in the act.

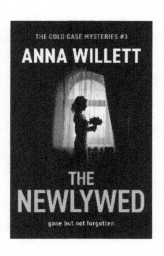

THE COLD CASE MYSTERIES #3

ANNA WILLETT

THE
NEWLYWED

gone but not forgotten

THE NEWLYWED by Anna Willett

When newlywed Jane Wilson disappeared many years ago,
her husband immediately fell under suspicion. But all the
police had was his testimony and no evidence. Examining
the cold case, Detective Pope has a hunch that Jane was
witness to a serious crime. Something dragged her back to
Seabreak and made sure she would never leave. And
whatever that was, may well be alive and ready to act again.

Made in United States
Orlando, FL
26 January 2024

42909856R00129